Stay For ~~while~~ Forever

D. E. Haggerty

Chapter 1

Why do all dogs go to heaven but not all people? Because people are jerks. Plain and simple.

As I LOOK AROUND the garden at the entire town of Winter Falls celebrating the love my sister, Ellery, has found, it's all I can do to not roll my eyes. Love. Ha! I thought I found it, but I was a naïve fool.

I can only hope the love my sister and her brand-spanking-new fiancé, Cole, share will last longer than my attempts at a happily ever after.

My phone buzzes in my pocket. Oh goodie. A reminder of why love sucks. Because I needed a reminder.

You'd think Mr. 'Can't buy a hint if it slaps him in the face' would have figured it out by now. We are over. Although, we never actually began. It's hard to have a relationship when half of the couple bolts the morning after sex. And leaving me alone in bed isn't the worst part. Not by a long shot.

"Here." Another one of my sisters – Aspen this time – presses a glass into my hand.

I sniff the drink and nearly rear back at the strong scent of alcohol. "What is this?"

"A martini."

A martini doesn't burn my nose hairs. "This is not a martini."

"Yes, it is. Gin and vodka equals martini." My book-obsessed sister always did suck at math.

I shiver. "What about the vermouth?"

"Trust me. You're going to need the fortification."

I pause with my lips on the glass. "What are you talking about?"

"It's your turn."

"My turn?"

My two other sisters, Lilac and Ashlyn, join us. Yep. There are five of us in total. I'd feel sorry for my poor father, but Dad loves his girls more than anything on earth.

"I believe she means she's going to meddle in your love life next," Lilac says.

Uh oh. My sisters have been falling for men like flies over the past year. First, Aspen returned to Winter Falls after her bookstore in Dallas burned down and rekindled her romance with her first love, Lyric. Afterwards, Ashlyn went balls to the wall to convince her forever crush, Rowan, to give her a chance. They're married now.

And, last but not least, Ellery got pregnant during a one-night stand with Cole. My stubborn sister gave the man a run for his money, but she accepted his marriage proposal today, so I'm thinking the running's over.

But my sisters being all loved up doesn't mean I want to be. I tried doing the whole love and romance thing. It was a disaster. Complete and utter disaster.

I retreat a step. "What about you?" I point to Lilac, the only other sister who remains unattached. "Why can't Aspen meddle in your love life?"

"Please," Aspen draws out the word. "I think we all know Lilac will be the last of us to pair off, and she's going to need the most help. It's for the best if all of us are happily paired off before we set our sights on matching Lilac."

"What if I don't want to be happily paired off?"

Ashlyn barks out a laugh. "Ha! Liar."

"I am not lying." I sneer at her.

I'm done with men. Men who make tons of promises before they get you in their bed but disappear before you wake up the next morning. Men who can't be bothered to answer your messages until you start ignoring them. I hate games. In fact, I'm thinking I hate most people at the moment.

I'll stick to my animals, thank you very much. My sweet pets never forget about me, and I never question how much they love me, because they show me how much they love me constantly.

The crowd buzzes, and I glance over at the back porch expecting to see Ellery and Cole emerge from the house. It's about time. But the happy couple is still missing from their own party.

"Someone's not a secret admirer anymore," Ashlyn sings. What is my baby sister – aka shit stirrer of the worst kind – talking about?

I scan the crowd and flaming ducks! I blink my eyes hoping I'm in the midst of some type of hallucination, but when my vision clears the scene in front of me hasn't changed. Maverick Langston is here. In my sister's backyard. Love a duck.

Aspen stares at him with her mouth hanging open as he stalks across the lawn toward us. I can't blame her for staring. My reaction the first time I met the owner of the Wildlife Refuge I manage wasn't much different.

You don't expect a Hollywood movie star to own a Wildlife Refuge in Winter Falls, Colorado – the town that defines the word quirky. Seriously. Our claim to fame is being the first carbon neutral town in the world, but the quirkiness doesn't stop there. Not even close.

But Maverick Langston is indeed the owner of the Wildlife Refuge. He's also a gorgeous movie star. Duh. Movie stars in general are gorgeous. He could have stepped directly off the silver screen with his thick brown hair, high cheekbones, and smoldering blue eyes.

Dang him. Why can't he have a big, fat hairy mole on his crooked nose? Probably because he's not a witch, but you get what I'm saying.

"You knew about him?" Aspen asks Ashlyn before he reaches us.

"Of course. Juniper and I don't have secrets."

I snort. "She means she followed me to work and spied on me." As I said, Ashlyn's a troublemaker.

"Same thing."

"June Bug," Mav greets in his deep voice, and I nearly forget why I've been ignoring the man. He smirks and I remember. He's a movie star who's playing at being with me. He's not really interested in me as a person. Hell, he's not interested in the Wildlife Refuge except as a tax write-off.

I tag his hand and drag him toward the furthest edge of the yard.

"What are you doing here?" I hiss at him. "You've blown your cover."

I don't actually care if the whole town knows the movie star has a house here and owns the place where I work, but if he's worried about everyone knowing about him, maybe he'll go away and never come back. My heart squeezes at the thought. *No, heart. Stop it! We don't care about him!*

"No, he hasn't," Sage says before he can respond. "We've known Rickie owned the Wildlife Refuge since he bought it."

"Nothing is sacred in this town," I grumble despite not being surprised at Sage's declaration. The woman's ability to ferret out secrets is refined to an art form.

"Sacred refers to—"

I shove my palm in Lilac's direction. Lilac is Ms. Literal. Words should be used in their most basic sense without any form of exaggeration according to her. And if you don't follow her rules, she makes her disapproval known. Not now, sis. The last thing I need at this very moment is a lecture on the proper use of the word sacred.

"Can't you give us some space to have a private conversation?" I ask when I notice everyone has followed us.

"Why?" Aspen questions, her brow wrinkled in confusion.

"I've never met a movie star before. I want an autograph," Ashlyn adds.

I roll my eyes at her. "You're a big fat liar. Half of your college graduating class became movie stars."

I'm not exaggerating. Ashlyn studied drama in college. While she didn't run off to try her hand at being an actor in Hollywood, many of her fellow students did. And they made it big.

"I wouldn't say stars," she mumbles.

"Who is this man?" Lilac asks. If I weren't in the middle of freaking out, I'd laugh at her question. Naturally, my sister, who I worry is more robot than person, has no clue who this movie star is.

"It's Maverick Langston. If you'd been to any of Juniper's monthly movie nights, you'd recognize him," Ashlyn explains.

"Enough!" I shout loud enough for the entire town to hear me. "Everyone needs to back off before the revealing of secrets begins."

"I don't have any secrets," Sage, the leader of the town busybodies, claims.

I cock an eyebrow. "How about the time I saw you—"

"Let's give Juniper and Rickie some space," she says before I can finish tattling on her for the time I caught her spying on her friend Petal's house with a pair of binoculars.

I wait until Sage has herded everyone toward the house before I turn my attention to Mav. "Now, what can I do for you?"

"You can stop running away."

Me? I'm the one running away? He must be joking.

He reaches for me, but I bat his hands away. He sighs. "I'm done playing around Juniper. I want you. You want me. It's time to figure out where this can go."

I know exactly where it will go. It's this place I refer to as heartbreak city. Been there. Done that. Have a broken heart as a souvenir. Do I plan to return? Not on your life.

"Not interested," I tell him before marching away.

Chapter 2

How you treat animals tells me all I need to know about you.

I PEEK OUT OF the window one more time before I open the back door to slink out of my house. This is what my life has come to – sneaking around to avoid Maverick the movie star aka heartbreaking lying piece of donkey dung. How dare *he* come to Winter Falls claiming it's 'time to figure out where this thing between us will go'!

I growl in annoyance and my dog, Bark Twain, howls in response, which of course means my other dog, Indiana Bones, barks and my cat, Meowise, snarls.

"Shush, guys. You're ruining my whole sneaking out of the house thing."

Bark Twain's ears lift in confusion before he lets a fart rip. I try not to gag. I don't want him thinking there's something wrong with him, but there is. There most definitely is something wrong with this dog. It's not normal for those sorts of smells to come out of an animal. And I should know.

As manager of the Wildlife Refuge outside of town, I spend most of my time with animals. Many of which come to the refuge ill because they were adopted as pets by rich people when they were adorable fur babies. Apparently, rich people think it's okay to not only own wildlife but to feed them human food.

It's not okay. Trust me. Those poor animals arrive at the refuge with gastronomical distress you cannot imagine. It's enough to make me gag, and I can hold my sister Ashlyn's hair back while she barfs without blinking an eye.

"Okay, sweet things, time for Mama to go to work." I use my foot to push my dogs back while my cat glares at me for having the gall to abandon her with those heathens aka the dogs.

I manage to escape the house and shut the door without anyone losing a paw. Time to get to work. I hop on my bike and begin pedaling toward the refuge. A block later I slow down when I notice Forest, the owner of the pet store, *Unleashed,* waving me down.

"Good morning," he bellows, and I cringe before glancing around to double-check no one heard him. It's hard to pull off incognito when the residents of your town pride themselves on being a bunch of busybodies.

"Hey, Forest." I rest my bike on its kickstand and kneel down to pet his chipmunk. "Hey, Chip," I coo. "How are you doing?" The little guy chirps in response and jumps into my lap. I cuddle him close. He's too cute.

"He's missing his brother, Dale."

I glance up to respond and nearly fall on my ass when I realize Forest isn't wearing any pants or underwear for that matter. I should know better. The man hates wearing any type of clothing over his family jewels. Apparently, clothing restricts his cojones – his word, not mine. Definitely, not mine.

This is Winter Falls at its finest. They'll skewer you for having the gall to use a plastic bag, but stroll around without pants on? No worries. You go for it.

"Bring Chip to the house soon and the brothers can have a family reunion," I tell Forest.

I adopted Chip's brother Dale, but Ashlyn, who was living with me at the time, threw a conniption fit and claimed she'd move out if I adopted Chip, too. I should have ignored her – to hell with her portion of the rent money – especially since she moved out a month later anyway.

Out of the corner of my eye, I notice someone in a bright pink sweater marching in our direction. Uh oh. The gossip gals wear bright pink sweaters. Those five women have been sticking their noses in my business ever since they found out Maverick and I had a 'thing'. I am not handing out details. No one needs to know what a naïve fool I was.

Time to get out of here before the gossip hounds of Winter Falls attack. I jump to my feet.

"I need to get to work. Later!" I hop on my bike and pedal off before Forest can respond.

"Juniper Berry, I know you saw me!"

I ignore Sage's yell. Sage is the police dispatcher in town. She's also the leader of the gossip gal gang and as such is the biggest gossip this side of the Mississippi. Correction. This side of the Atlantic. I wish I were exaggerating.

I breathe a sigh of relief when I arrive at the Wildlife Refuge. This place isn't only a refuge for the animals, but it's my refuge as well. It's the one place in town where I can have a bit of peace. Where none of my sisters come barging after me, and none of the busybodies bother me.

The animals at this Wildlife Refuge are 'unique'. We specialize in animals people thought would make good pets but in fact, don't. But the 'people' I'm referring to aren't any old people. No, they're mostly Hollywood stars because 'he who shall not be named' is a movie star and has 'connections'. I'll show you what I think of his connections.

I notice the light in the capybara shelter is on. Uh oh. Did I leave it on? I'm usually meticulous in ensuring everything at the refuge is perfect for my babies before I go home. But I have an intern who in addition to covering weekends comes over for a few hours at night to check up on the animals. Maybe Harmony forgot to switch off a light?

I make my way to the shelter where we have several capybaras. The giant rodents look like a mix between a cavy and a guinea pig. In other words, they're beyond adorable. They're also affectionate, making people think they're great pets, except they don't respond well to being alone. But do people listen and ensure their pet capybara has a buddy? Of course not.

I enter the enclosure and freeze when I see Maverick. Damn it. Maverick Langston the movie star aka 'he who flees in the morning before the girl wakes' aka 'the jerk' is here in my sanctuary. How dare he? Yeah. Yeah. I know he owns the place, but he never comes here except to check the books twice a year.

And why does he have to show up appearing positively delectable? His thick brown hair is tousled perfectly making me want to shove my hands through it and mess it all up. And then there's his model perfect high cheekbones and square jaw hidden under his trimmed beard. Add in his smoldering blue eyes and the picture equals yowzah! There's a reason the man is everyone's favorite romantic lead.

I shake my head and all thoughts of licking his abs from it. The last thing I need is to lick one of Maverick 'only interested when the girl gets fed up with you' Langston's body parts.

"What the hell are you doing here?"

He flashes me his Hollywood smile. The one I fell for too many times to count. Well, no more. This girl has learned her lesson, and I got an A+ on the final exam.

His smile falters for a millisecond before it intensifies. "I'm helping you."

My hands land on my hips. "Helping me? You haven't the first hint of a clue how to help me."

"How hard can it be?"

I growl. Is he saying anyone could do my job? And my master's in Biology is superfluous? I guess I won't be paying back the mountain of student debt I incurred since my degree is worthless.

He smirks at me, and I decide it's time to teach Mr. Hollywood a lesson. I cross my arms over my chest and nod toward the enclosure. "Go ahead. It's time for the capybaras to go swimming."

He opens the door, and it swings open. Instead of allowing the animals to waddle to the water for some pool time on their own, he reaches in and grabs one.

"I wouldn't—"

He shushes me. "These guys are adorable. What could possibly go wrong?"

Because it's always smart to hold a baby animal while the mamma is growling at you. He turns away from the growling mamma. Big mistake.

I step forward. "Seriously, Mav, you need to put her down."

"Why? Are you jealous someone else is cuddling me?" He winks.

Could he be a bigger ass? Is he seriously making light of my jealousy? How dare he? He struts around with Hollywood starlets and kisses them in front of the entire world after sneaking away from my bed. Of course, I'm jealous. I'm a red-blooded, heterosexual woman. Calling me on my jealousy proves what a jerk he is.

"You need to put her down, Maverick," I order.

He doesn't listen to me. He never does. Instead, he lifts the rodent up to his face and begins baby talking it.

"June Bug is grumpy in the morning, isn't she?"

He'd know I'm grumpy in the morning if he had stuck around after talking his way into my bed and my pants. *Enough, Juniper! E-freaking-nough!* Stop living in the past. There will never be a Juniper and Maverick – obviously. I'd be a fool to stay with a man who sneaks out of my bed. He's merely here now because I've been ignoring him, and no vain man enjoys being ignored.

He nuzzles the creature. I step forward to snatch the baby from his arms, but he tuts at me before twirling around. Ugh! I know the man is a pompous ass. I didn't realize he's a complete and utter idiot, too.

"She's going to—"

Before I manage to warn him again, he screeches and drops the baby.

"She bit me! She fucking bit me."

His hand covers his nose. The rest of the capybaras gather at his feet chittering at him. When he glances down and notices them, he retreats.

"Go away, you little devils!" he screeches.

I reach for him. "Calm down. Let me check the bite."

"They're attacking me."

I roll my eyes. "They're not attacking you. Stop being a baby."

"I'm not a baby." He waves a hand toward the capybaras at his feet. "These animals appear cute, but they are utterly ferocious."

He glares down at them, and they grunt and whistle at him. His eyes widen. "Are they planning to attack me?"

Was he always such a pansy? They're rodents. Adorable rodents.

He holds up his hands as he backs away.

"Watch where you're—"

Before I manage to get the warning out, he falls backward into the pool. The capybaras jump in after him, and his arms flail as he attempts to avoid them.

"I guess it's a good thing you're not an action hero," I say and offer him my hand.

He ignores me and hops out of the pool on his own. His shirt is soaked and clinging to his chest. Each and every striation of his chest muscles is outlined by the material. My mouth waters. I know how smooth and warm those muscles are. They're infinitely lick-able.

He smirks. "Notice anything you fancy?" His words remind me of what a scumbag he is.

"Nope. Just checking your shirt isn't ripped from the capybaras 'attacking' you."

He shudders. "I'm going to…" He doesn't bother finishing his sentence before he scurries out of the enclosure.

I don't wait until he's gone before I let the laugh I've been containing roar out of me.

"Good job, sweet things. We won't be seeing him anytime soon."

And, no, those words don't cause my stomach to sour. Nope. I am done with Maverick Langston. D. O. N. E. Done.

Chapter 3

At what age is it appropriate to tell my dog he's adopted?

"Don't go in there!"

I groan when Ashlyn's whisper-shout wakes me.

"Why not? We've checked every other area of the house. Juniper must be in her bedroom."

"You'll be sorry," Ashlyn sings.

"Are you being sarcastic?" I can practically hear Lilac's brow wrinkle as she tries to ascertain whether Ashlyn's being sarcastic or not. Lilac doesn't understand sarcasm. I'm half-positive she's an artificial intelligence experiment gone wrong, because who doesn't understand sarcasm?

The door to my bedroom opens for a second before it slams closed again.

"Are you crazy? She has a snake in there."

"I'm positive Juniper doesn't have a snake slithering around on her floor," Lilac says before opening the door again and switching on the lights. "There's no snake here, but there is a terrarium."

I frown. The terrarium is empty. Slinky no longer lives there. He freaked the cat out and the dogs barked at him constantly.

As much as I loved Slinky and how much his presence in my house kept my baby sister away, I had to give him up.

Ashlyn squeals and scrambles away. "I don't want to know! I don't want to know!"

I sigh before flinging my covers off and standing and following her to the living room where all four of my sisters are gathered. Awesome. "What are you doing here?"

Lilac frowns. "According to Ashlyn, we're here to get the gossip. According to Aspen, we're here to sort your shit." Literal Lilac strikes again!

"I'm here because I'm a gazillion months pregnant, and my fiancé has become Mr. Overprotective. I needed a break."

Ellery grunts as she rubs her stomach, but there's one of those secret smiles on her face. Her baby daddy proposed to her a few days ago after he bought her the house of her dreams. I wasn't sold on Cole when I found out he'd knocked my sister up after a one-night stand, but anyone who can get my stubborn sister to take a break from the inn she manages is a hero in my book. Because my sister is the definition of workaholic when it comes to her baby, *The Inn on Main.*

"Did someone at least bring refreshments?" I ask as I plop down on a chair. Dale skitters into the room and jumps onto my lap.

"This is not a refreshment visit. We didn't stop by for a chat," Aspen proclaims.

"We didn't?" Ashlyn wrinkles her nose. "I want all the gossip. How long have you been involved with the movie star Maverick Langston?" She wiggles her eyebrows.

My stomach sours at the mention of his name. "We're not involved."

She giggles. "It looked like you were involved when—"

"Enough!" I order, causing my dogs to come racing out of my bedroom to find me while barking and howling. Great. My neighbor will be complaining about my animals again.

Bark Twain springs onto the chair causing my chipmunk to jump on my shoulder. I try not to wince when I feel his nails dig into my skin. Not to be outdone, Indiana Bones sticks his snout on my leg. I dig my hand in his fur and scratch him behind the ears.

As soon as my animals settle – no need to worry about Meowise as she'll be taking over the bed with her rivals gone – I confront Ashlyn. "It's not okay to play super sleuth and follow me around before spying in the window." I can feel my face heat at the reminder of what she saw as I glare at her.

She shrugs. "If you had told me what you were up to, I wouldn't have needed to sneak around."

"Welcome to my life," Aspen mutters. "She followed Lyric and me around like a lost puppy dog when we were in high school."

Lyric and Aspen were inseparable in high school. Everyone was convinced they'd get married straight out of college. Unfortunately, they lost their way for a while there, but they're engaged now and disgustingly in love. Gag.

"You have your own husband now. Why don't you go home and play with him instead of interfering in my life?" I suggest to Ashlyn.

She does one of those dreamy sighs I thought were made up by Hollywood. She's been in love with Rowan forever. It took her breaking an ankle and taking a jackhammer to his walls, but she finally broke him down and now they too are disgustingly in love.

Don't get me wrong. I'm happy three of my sisters have found love. Good for them, but I am done with men. I should probably form an alliance with Lilac because there's no way my robotic sister will ever fall in love.

Lilac consults her watch. "Can we hurry this discussion along? I have an early morning meeting I can't be late for." Lilac is an environmental engineer, but you'd think she was a doctor making life and death decisions with how seriously she takes her work.

"Can't be late because the person you're meeting is hot?" Ashlyn asks.

Ellery laughs. "Are you joking? This is Lilac we're talking about. She wouldn't know a hot guy if he hit her in the face."

"Hit me in the face? Why would anyone hit me in the face?" Lilac asks, but I notice her cheeks are pink.

Please don't tell me she's in love now, too. I'm going to be the crazy cat lady in the family. I glance down at the dogs in my lap. Amendment. The crazy dog lady.

Aspen claps to get our attention, and Bark Twain and Indiana Bones yip at her. I pet them until they calm down.

"Can we get to the point now?" She phrases her words as a question, but there's no doubt in my mind it's a demand.

"What is the point?" I ask as if I don't know.

She throws her hands in the air. "How the hell did we not know you're having an affair with a freaking movie star?"

"One, I'm not having an affair with him." Nope. That ship has sailed.

Ellery snorts. "Who do you think you're fooling? Maverick Langston showed up at my engagement party and said – and I quote here – I want you. You want me. It's time to figure out where this can go."

"Can we stop swooning over the 'movie star'?" Ashlyn responds before I have a chance. "He's not the only famous person in the world you know. I am married to a former football player who has a Super Bowl ring."

I ignore her to confront Ellery. "How the hell do you know what he said to me? You were still in the house when he arrived."

She blushes and dips her chin to avoid my gaze.

I wag my finger at her. "Nuh-uh. No way. You're not ignoring me now. Tell me or I'll puppy nap Honey."

Honey is the puppy I gave Ellery at her baby shower. Everyone thought the gift was 'inappropriate', but who did she turn to when she thought Cole had left her? You got it. Her adorable puppy. And seriously, what did anyone expect me to gift her? I don't have the first clue what a pregnant woman needs or wants.

She gasps. "You wouldn't dare."

I cock my eyebrow. "Try me."

"Sage told me," she mutters.

My eyes widen. "The same Sage who said she'd give me space to talk to Mav?"

Sage is the bane of my existence. If she weren't a million years old, I'd teach her a lesson I refer to as 'these cookies were made with puppy chow and not oats'. That'd show her.

"She calls him Mav," is Ashlyn's bizarre response. "They're totally bumping uglies."

I narrow my eyes at her. "We are not bumping uglies."

"Doing the horizontal tango, going to bone town, getting a hole in one… whatever you want to call it."

I wouldn't call it any of those things because, unlike my baby sister, I'm not a permanent member of crazy town.

"How can I say this in a way you can understand? Maverick Langston and I are not involved." I speak slowly and enunciate every syllable.

"I understand perfectly." Lilac stands. "Are we finished with whatever this is? I need to get at least seven hours of sleep. I prefer eight, obviously, as eight hours of sleep is the optimum to maintain good health."

Ashlyn groans. "Someone save me from a lecture from Ms. Know It All about proper sleeping etiquette."

Ellery tries to stand. "A lecture on sleep etiquette is better than a gazillion lectures on what I can and cannot eat and what I can and cannot do."

Lilac frowns as she extends her hand to help the very pregnant Ellery stand. "You do know 'gazillion' is not an actual measurement, don't you?"

"Yes, Ms. Scientific America, it's an exaggeration used for emphasis."

Aspen ignores the hubbub around her as she studies me. I hold my breath and force myself not to squirm. After several long seconds, she smirks. "This is going to be fun."

Uh oh. My big sis thinks she's going to play matchmaker again. As the oldest West sister and the first to be engaged, she thinks she has the right to couple all of her sisters. I open my mouth to tell her to mind her own business, but I slam it shut before I can utter a word. I'm not giving her any fuel for the matchmaker fire.

I stand and follow my sisters to the door. "I want my key back, Ashlyn."

Ashlyn rolls her eyes before digging it out of her pocket. "Not having a key won't stop me from breaking in again."

There's no response to her craziness. I shut the door in her face without comment before collapsing against it. Maybe I should find somewhere else to live while Mav's in town. I could stay with Mom and Dad. They'd never turn me away. Bark Twain leans against my legs to offer me comfort.

Darn. Mom and Dad may be okay with me staying with them, but they won't let me bring my animals. Mom is strangely fussy about animals and their shedding. And Dad? Let's just say after the one time I 'accidentally' brought a snake home, animals and him have not been friends.

Guess I'll have to put up with my sisters' visits. They won't last long anyway since Mav never stays in town for long. This time won't be any different no matter what he claims to the contrary. I've heard his claims before. They're hot air and nothing more.

Chapter 4

Letting the cat out of the bag is a whole lot easier than putting it back in.

MAVERICK

"Here," the waiter says before setting a large coffee down on the table in front of me, "you're going to need this."

I wrinkle my brow. "I am?"

He chuckles. "You're meeting the gossip gals. Of course, you do."

"I'm not meeting the gossip gals." I don't even know who the gossip gals are.

He snorts. "I'm Bryan. Tug on your ear if you need saving."

Is he serious? "Um, okay," I agree, and he flounces away.

Winter Falls is weird. Don't get me wrong. I love the quirky Colorado town where the environment is more important than wearing pants. I'm not joking no matter how much I wish I were. But to each their own.

And when I say to each their own, I mean it. No one in town bothers me. I thought it was because I was disguising my presence, but it turns out everyone in town knows I own the Wildlife Refuge. They also know I've been coming to town off and on for years now. And yet I haven't been asked for my autograph once. It's refreshing.

I'm relieved the town doesn't go gaga over my star status as I plan to be in town a lot more in the future. As soon as I convince Juniper Berry West I'm the man for her, Winter Falls will officially be my home. The bell above the door to the bakery, *Bake Me Happy,* rings and Sage walks in. Time to instigate my plan to convince Juniper to give me a chance.

Several women file in after Sage. They're all wearing bright pink t-shirts with the words *Gossip Gal Matchmaker* on them. As I watch, they follow Sage to my table.

"Um…" I'm rarely at a loss for words – thank you Hollywood publicists – but how do you respond to a group of elderly women showing up uninvited? Wearing shirts declaring themselves matchmakers? I was expecting Sage to join me this morning, not a whole crew of interfering busybodies. Maybe I do need to tug on my ear.

Sage snaps her fingers. "Bryan! We need more chairs."

Bryan rushes over and helps everyone get seated. He winks at me before whispering, "Told you so."

I sip on my coffee for fortification. "What are all of you doing here?"

Sage doesn't answer my question and says instead, "Let's begin with the introductions, shall we?"

"To my right is Feather." The woman winks at me.

"Next to her is Petal." She bites her lip and flutters her lashes at me. "When the time comes, she'll help you with the appropriate sex candles."

I gulp. Sex candles?

"On my other side are Cayenne and Clove. Clove's off limits since she's been married to the same man for thirty years."

Off limits? Who do they think I am? Some carouser? I won't lie and say I didn't enjoy a smorgasbord of women in the years after my second movie became a hit, but those days are done. They were done the minute I laid eyes on Juniper. Too bad it took me a while to realize what I had with her.

Juniper is hands down the sexiest woman I've ever seen. She's a few inches shorter than me and fits me perfectly. She may be thin from all the running around with animals she does – not to mention she forgets to eat way too often – but she has curves in all the best places. Curves my mouth is dying to explore once again.

Without a doubt, her face could fill a Hollywood screen. She has these cat-like green eyes that intrigue me to no end. And her full lips make me want to bite her bottom lip before soothing it over with my tongue. She rarely wears her hair down but when she does, her long brown curly hair is as gorgeous as the rest of her.

The sound of coffee mugs hitting the table breaks me out of my fantasy of fisting Juniper's hair while I devour her mouth.

Bryan tugs on his ear before abandoning me. At least someone's having fun.

"Now, where are we at?" Sage asks.

"Excuse me, where are we at?" I repeat her question because I've lost the plot.

"With project MavBerry."

I must have heard her wrong. "MavBerry?"

"Did you not know Juniper's middle name is Berry?" She doesn't wait for my response before pulling a notebook out of her enormous bag as she informs me, "I have some ideas. Shall we discuss them?"

What was I thinking? Why did I set up a meeting with Sage? My idea was to feel her out, make certain she was on my side. Not discuss ideas regarding MavBerry. Whatever the hell that is.

"I believe the biggest issue is convincing Juniper you're in town to stay." She pauses to stare at me. "You are here to stay, aren't you?"

I squirm in my seat. "Yes, ma'am."

She purses her lips. "You're not going to run off the second you get a better offer?"

"A better offer?"

"You know. One of those Hollywood starlets. They may appear pretty on the silver screen, but no one can hold a candle to our Juniper Berry."

It finally hits me. MavBerry. It's a portmanteau aka blended name of Maverick and Berry. Juniper is going to lose her mind when she hears it. I grin. Juniper is sexy as hell when she's mad.

"No," I tell the women. "No one in Hollywood is on the same level as Juniper."

Sage nods her approval, and the other women murmur their agreement.

"I think he should do a grand gesture," Cayenne offers.

"Good idea. What kind of grand gesture?" Feather asks.

"He could get her name tattooed on his arm," Clove suggests.

I cringe. Although many Hollywood stars have tattoos, they're a pain in the ass to have when shooting a film. I have no desire to wear an inch of make-up to hide a tattoo – computer graphics can't hide everything. Besides, it's kind of creepy getting a woman's name tattooed on you when you aren't dating, although we will be dating – soon.

"And ruin his perfect skin?" Sage asks but doesn't wait for anyone to answer her. "No. Any other ideas?"

"He could serenade her under her window," Petal suggests. "We could put candles all around him and make it super romantic."

"The last time you decided to use candles outside, we had to call the Fire Department before you burned the entire forest down," Sage reminds her.

Petal shrugs. "River didn't seem to mind."

"Who's River?" I ask in a blatant attempt to change the topic of discussion.

"Lyric's brother," Clove answers.

"And who's Lyric?" It's as if they're talking a foreign language I don't speak.

"He's your soon-to-be brother-in-law."

Sage's answer totally cleared things up. Not. I frown at her.

She sighs. "Lyric is Aspen's fiancé. I assume you know who Aspen is."

Finally, a name I recognize. Aspen is Juniper's oldest sister. I've never met any of her family, but Juniper talked about her sisters all the time. As an only child of parents who are more interested in my wealth than they are in me, I can admit I'm a bit jealous of her relationship with her siblings.

"I do."

"A grand gesture is a good idea," Sage begins, "but based on Juniper's reaction to Rickie at Ellery's engagement party, I don't think Juniper is ready for a grand gesture."

I release the breath I didn't realize I was holding. Don't get me wrong. I'm all for grand gestures. In movies where they belong. Juniper is not the type of woman who wants a grand gesture. She wants me to show up. Which is exactly what I tried to do yesterday at the Wildlife Refuge. It's not my fault I didn't realize those rodents were mean fuckers.

"I have another idea," Sage says, and whatever relief I was feeling flies out the window.

Feather rubs her hands together. "What is it? Does it involve ice cream and lots of naked skin?"

Cayenne rolls her eyes. "Feather owns the ice cream shop, *Feather's Frozen Delights*."

"Really?" I raise a brow. "The ice cream there is fabulous."

Feather tucks her chin into her chest but not before I note the pink painting her cheeks. "Thank you."

"Ahem." Sage clears her throat. "Can we return to my idea now?"

I motion for her to go ahead. It's not as if I can stop whatever's going to come out of her mouth anyway.

"You need to show Juniper you're here to stay and what better way for you to show her your intentions than to get involved in the community."

Since the community is completely wacko, I'm afraid of whatever idea she's concocted.

She smiles. "For instance, you could involve yourself in one of our community activities."

Is she purposely talking in riddles? "What community activity did you have in mind?"

Her smile switches into a smirk. "What better activity for the Hollywood star than movie night?"

I do know a lot about movies. "What do you need me to do? Pick the movie? Arrange for its arrival? What?"

Sage raises her hand and snaps her fingers. "Bryan, we need sustenance."

"I've got exactly what you need." He wiggles his eyebrows in my direction. "Chocolate and coffee coming up."

I gulp. I'm either making the biggest mistake of my life or this is my first step toward getting Juniper to accept the idea of there being an us. I hope it's the latter.

Chapter 5

Life's a bitch and she just had puppies.

I ENTER THE LIBRARY and come to a screeching halt at the vision in front of me. What's happening here? Tonight is movie night – a monthly event I'm in charge of. I spend the better part of each month dodging people's questions about what the movie of the month will be. It's too much fun to throw the gossip gals off the scent.

This month's movie is a classic – *Casablanca* – because there is no way in hell I'm watching a movie where the guy gets the girl in the end. Nope. Happy endings are complete bullshit.

But now is not the time to think about how ridiculous and completely inaccurate happy endings are, because right now I've got a problem. A problem as in everyone's already here. I check my watch. As usual, I'm thirty minutes early. Normally, I arrive early to set up the chairs and get the movie cued up. Why is everyone else here ahead of schedule?

I scan the crowd and my gaze lands on Ashlyn sitting with her husband Rowan. She gives me two thumbs up. Great. My baby sister is doing what she does best – causing trouble.

Aspen arrives and tries to march past me, but I grab her arm to stop her. "What's going on? Why is everyone early?"

Her eyes roam the room in a blatant attempt to avoid my gaze. "Early? What are you talking about?"

Wow. Someone sucks at lying. Before I have a chance to call her on her lies, her fiancé Lyric appears and pulls her away from me. I let him. Lyric might be my future brother-in-law, but he's also the Chief of Police of Winter Falls. I'm not getting on his bad side. When your baby sister can find trouble in a convent – don't ask – you learn to keep the police on your side.

"Ahem. May I have your attention?"

No way. I close my eyes and pray. *Please tell me I'm hearing things. Please tell me it's not Maverick standing in front of the town introducing the movie. Please. Please. Please.*

"This month's movie is a classic."

My eyes fly open. Maybe I'm exaggerating things.

Mav's gaze meets mine. "It's a classic tale of a man falling in love with a woman except the woman isn't any old woman. She's a movie star."

A movie star? Ilsa Lund, played by Ingrid Bergman, isn't a movie star in *Casablanca.* What the hell is he up to?

"Many of you are probably familiar with this film." He pauses for dramatic effect. "*Notting Hill.*"

Notting Hill is not this month's movie selection. My jaw clenches, and I glare at Mav.

"Payback's a bitch," Aspen hollers.

"Not the same thing, big sis."

And it's not. Aspen and Lyric were on a date and finding their way back to each other when I chose *Sweet Home Alabama* as the monthly movie. I freely admit I was insinuating Aspen – like Melanie Smooter in the movie – was still in love with Lyric and should stay in her hometown when I chose the movie.

But this situation is completely different. Mav and I are not in the middle of some great love affair. He used me for booty calls in the past and that's it. He's not in love with me. Hell, we're not even friends. At most, we're employer and employee.

"Who thinks Juniper should give Maverick a chance?" Ashlyn shouts her question, and every single person in the room raises their hand.

"Who thinks Juniper should have a say in who she dates?" I shout back and search the crowd for my dad.

If no one else will stand up for me, Dad will. He may be a laid back hippie but no one – and I do mean no one – messes with his girls.

"Dad's not here," Aspen says as if she can read my mind. Since she knows exactly who I'm searching for, I guess she kind of can. She smirks before continuing. "He and Mom are having a night in. Hint. Hint. Nudge. Nudge."

Ashlyn gags. "La. La. La. I can't hear you."

As much fun as it is to watch Ashlyn be uncomfortable – especially considering she's the one usually causing the uncomfortableness – I am not interested in a discussion about my parents' sex life. They have one. I don't need to know more.

"Shall we roll the movie?" Mav asks the crowd, and I lose it.

"No! *We* aren't rolling the movie. *Notting Hill* is not the movie *I* picked out for this month's movie night. And since *I'm* in charge of movie night, we need to switch out the movies."

"I already sent *Casablanca* back."

"You did what?" I screech at such a volume I probably woke all the animals at the Wildlife Refuge two miles out of town up.

"I have five dollars on Juniper kicking him in the nuts," Ashlyn hollers, and I turn my glare on her.

She shrugs. "What? My money's on you."

"Make it ten and you're on," Forest yells from the back of the room.

"You're betting against me? I'm your best customer."

"Actually, Maverick here is the owner of the Wildlife Refuge, which makes *him* my best customer."

"Are you kidding me? He bought the refuge as a tax write-off. I'm the one who's there every day taking care of the animals."

"Hey now. I didn't buy it solely as a tax write-off," Mav says and interrupts my stare down with Forest.

"Enough! You don't get to waltz into Winter Falls and take over. This is my town, my home. You don't belong here."

"Hey!" Sage yells. "There's no excuse for being mean."

"Me?" I pound my chest with a fist. "I'm the mean one? I'm the one who sweet talked my way into Mav's bed only to leave in the morning to be with another woman?"

Sage gasps. "Oh, Rickie, say you didn't."

"June Bug, it's not what it looked like."

I snort. "And how many times have you told me those exact same words? How stupid do you think I am?"

"I don't think you're stupid. I think you're smart and gorgeous."

"This is better than the movie," Ashlyn says as she munches on popcorn.

Son of a dog. What am I doing airing my dirty laundry for everyone to see, hear, and smell? As if life isn't a bag of spoiled puppy chow already.

I whirl on my heel and without a word, I stomp out of the library. Screw movie night. Mav can have it. He'll be gone by next month anyway. The man never stays in town long.

"June Bug, wait!"

I ignore Mav and hurry in the direction of the brewery. Beer and nachos are exactly what the doctor ordered. Hopefully, most of the town residents will be at movie night, and I'll be allowed to eat in peace.

Mav dashes in front of me and stops – forcing me to come to a halt in the middle of the sidewalk. "Please, June Bug, talk to me."

"Talk to you?" I snarl. "The same way you talked to me all those times I wanted to talk to you, and you left without a word?"

He flinches. "I deserved that."

Hell, yeah, he did.

He reaches for me, but I bat his hands away.

"I have nothing to talk to you about."

I step into the street to go around him. It's not as if I need to worry about a car running me over. As the first carbon neutral town in the world, we in Winter Falls pride ourselves on there being no cars in our streets. Bikes and golf carts are our main source of transportation. Neither of which do I need to worry about crashing into me.

"I'm not giving up, June Bug."

I snort. "Yeah, you will. You'll get bored and go back to Hollywood, the same as always. Except this time, I won't be stupid enough to let you talk me into getting in bed with you."

"I'm not some sleaze who used you for sex."

"You're not? You didn't sleep with me and disappear in the morning before I woke up?"

"I got called away."

I roll my eyes. "And what? You couldn't wake me and tell me or, I don't know, write a note. There are these things called paper and pencil. Very handy and low tech. You'll find the objects in most households."

"I tried phoning you," he claims, and I notice several people peeking around the entrance of the library. Great. I've always wanted my heartbreak to become fodder for the town's gossip.

I snort. "A week later after I ignored your text messages. You don't want me. You want me because you can no longer have me. Go home."

"I am home."

I cross my arms over my chest and watch as his eyes dip to the cleavage revealed by the action. When his gaze returns to mine, his eyes are heated. Dang it. Why does his attraction to my body make me feel all warm and gooey inside? I'm not a stupid marshmallow.

"No, you're not. You belong in Hollywood with the rest of the A-listers. Not in Winter Falls."

"What if I want to belong here?"

"You'll be bored before the month is out."

"I accept your wager. What do I get when I win?"

"This is not a joke," I hiss at him. "This is my life, my family, my hometown."

He sighs. "I know. What I don't know is how to convince you this is my home now, too."

"You sound like you're trying to convince yourself."

He winces, and I know I'm correct. This isn't the place for Maverick Langston. Too bad I didn't come to the realization before my heart latched onto the man. No, not my heart. I was never in love with Mav. In lust? Totally. In love? Nope. I don't know the man. How could I love him? And I'm not a big, fat liar either.

"I'll see you around, Mav," I say before speed walking away. This time when he yells my name, I keep on going. Talking to him won't resolve our issues.

Chapter 6

MAVERICK

I wave at the bartender and tap my glass to indicate I'm ready for a refill. I've turned into the cliché romance hero. I'm drinking my sorrows away at the local bar, although this local bar isn't similar to anything I've ever seen before. If I had to describe it, I'd say someone threw up all things hippie related in here.

The walls are covered in posters and other paraphernalia from the peak of the hippie revolution. There isn't a matching chair in the place and colored lights decorate the walls and ceiling. I'm blaming the dazzling lights for making me see double because being drunk would make me even more of a cliché.

Someone slaps my back before grabbing my shoulder and hauling me off my stool.

"What are you doing?" I ask as I stumble to my feet.

"Uh-oh. The po-po has arrived," the bartender grumbles.

I squint up at the man grasping my shoulder. "I didn't do it, officer," I say. Or, at least, I think I say those words. Judging by the confusion marring his face, I wasn't as clear as I thought I was.

"Come on." He drags me away from the bar and shoves me into a booth.

"Why are we sitting in a booth? Aren't we going to kidnap him?" another man asks.

"Dude, he's famous. We can't kidnap him. Someone will miss him," a third man says. I study him. He's at least a half foot taller than six-foot with wide shoulders. If he's here to kidnap me, I'm in big trouble.

"But it was perfectly acceptable to kidnap me?"

The big guy shrugs.

"Fucker."

"What's going on?" I ask before they can continue their discussion about kidnapping me, which is frankly freaking me out.

"Drink this." The police officer slams a glass of water down in front of me.

"Yes, sir." I gulp the water down in one go. "All done," I declare as I put the glass down in front of me. "Now, can you explain what I did wrong, officer?"

The big guy chuckles. "Officer? Now there's a term you don't hear very often anymore."

I narrow my eyes and concentrate on him. "Do I know you?" His face is familiar. I know I've seen him before, but I don't think he's a Hollywood star. There aren't too many actors who are as big as him. Hold up. I know who he is.

"You're Rowan Hansley." As in former NFL quarterback, Rowan Hansley.

He grins and holds out his hand. "Nice to meet you."

"Maverick Langston," I say my name as we shake hands. "The NFC championship game a few years ago. Your throw in the last ten seconds for a touchdown. Ninety-five yards. Amazing."

It wasn't the longest football throw in the history of the NFL, but it came damn close. And it sealed the NFC championship for his team.

The police officer growls. "Are you two done kissing each other asses now?"

Rowan winks at him. "Don't be jealous because you're not famous."

"I'm not famous, and I'm not jealous," the third man claims.

"If you're not jealous, why do want to kidnap me?" I ask him.

He crosses his arms and glares at the other men. "Because these two kidnapped me when I got caught up with a West sister."

"A West sister? Juniper's family?"

"I'm Lyric," the police officer says.

"Aspen's fiancé?"

He nods as he offers his hand. "I'm also the Chief of Police."

His hand squeezes mine to the point of pain. "Message received."

The would-be kidnapper shakes my hand next. "Cole. Ellery's fiancé and baby daddy."

Baby daddy? Juniper's going to be an aunt? She never told me. Of course, there's a lot she hasn't told me considering I'm sitting across from three men who are involved with her sisters, and she never said a word to me about them.

"And I'm Ashlyn's husband," Rowan announces.

"The only one who could close the deal."

He smirks in response.

Lyric's eyes narrow on Rowan. "Yeah, because he snuck off to Vegas. Aspen's mom is pissed. There's no way the rest of the sisters will elope."

Cole bumps Lyric's shoulder. "But the chief has tried to drag Aspen off to Vegas more than once."

Lyric frowns at him. "And you haven't tried to convince Ellery to sneak off to the courthouse to get married? Don't think I don't know you applied for a marriage license."

"Small town gossip," Cole grumbles under his breath. "She's eight months pregnant. I want her to have my name before the baby's born. I don't think it's too much to ask."

"Dude, you literally got engaged a week ago. Give it time."

Cole frowns at Rowan. "What's with the dude-thing? Are we surfers now?"

"Sorry, Ashlyn's rubbing off on me." He waggles his brows. "Although, I don't mind her rubbing on me."

Lyric reaches across the table and slaps his shoulder. "You're talking about my sister."

"Speaking of sisters," Rowan begins.

"What the hell are you doing with Juniper?" Cole jumps in.

I rub my hand down my face. "I messed up."

Lyric shakes his head at me. "Ya think?"

I cringe. "It's not how it seemed."

Rowan growls. "You weren't seen with another woman the day after you slept with Juniper?"

My chin drops to my chest in defeat. "It was a publicity stunt."

He scoffs. "You should know better."

I want to lash out at him, but if there's anyone who understands how it feels to be under a microscope twenty-four/seven, it's him. I sigh. "I know."

"Doesn't look like a publicity stunt to me." Lyric passes me his phone, and I watch as the footage of the worst day of my life unfolds.

I'm holding the actress Quinn Wilder in my arms before I bend her backwards and lay a kiss on her. I always did have a flair for the dramatic – I am an actor after all – but I took it too far. I didn't need to kiss her to make the paparazzi believe we were together. The video ends, and I drop the phone on the table.

"I'm an idiot."

"If you're waiting for anyone to disagree with you, you're going to be waiting a long ass time," the bartender says as he sets a pitcher of beer and four glasses on the table.

"Does everyone in town know?" I whisper my question once he leaves.

"Yep." Cole opens his arms wide. "Welcome to small town living. It takes a bit to get used to."

"You're not from here?" I ask in a desperate attempt to change the subject.

"Nice try," Lyric says. He fills a glass with beer and slides it across the table to me. "You're not getting out of this discussion."

"Exactly. If we can't kidnap you, we can at least interrogate you."

"What is your obsession with kidnapping me?" I ask Cole.

"It's only fair since they." He motions toward Rowan and Lyric. "Kidnapped me after it came out I got Ellery pregnant."

"Stop being a wuss. We didn't harm you."

Cole's eyes widen at Lyric's statement. "What do you call pouring a bucket of freezing cold water over me?"

"A friendly warning."

His nostrils flare as he glares at Lyric. "I didn't need a warning. The second the word pregnant fell from Ellery's lips, I wasn't ever going to let her go."

"We needed to be certain."

Cole motions to me. "And how are we going to make certain Maverick is what Juniper wants and needs?"

Lyric shrugs. "Ask him."

Cole doesn't miss a beat. "How are you going to show Juniper you're serious?"

I hold up my hands as I shake my head. "Nuh-uh. No way. I'm not taking advice from any other Winter Falls residents. The last time I did, I ended up hurting Juniper's feelings."

Rowan laughs. "You should know better than to listen to advice from the Gossip Gals."

"I didn't even know who the Gossip Gals were and all of sudden they were sitting at a table with me telling me to make a grand gesture." I shiver.

Lyric smirks. "You can't deny grand gestures work."

"True." Rowan nods in agreement. "We all got a West sister by pulling off a grand gesture."

This town is obsessed with grand gestures. "Your advice is I make some kind of grand gesture?"

"No way. It's too early. Juniper isn't even talking to you. Any gesture you make now will be a waste," Cole explains.

"Exactly," Lyric agrees. "You need to get her to talk to you first."

"And how do I accomplish that?" I ask.

Lyric grins. "Leave it to us."

Since I don't have any better ideas, I agree. "Okay, but I won't be parading around town in my underwear with my chest all greased up."

Lyric smirks. "Don't worry. No underwear will be involved."

His reassurance is not putting me at ease whatsoever, but he knows Juniper and this town. It can't hurt to listen to him. Things between Juniper and I couldn't get any worse than they currently are.

My heart burns at the thought and I reach up to rub my chest. I hurt her bad, and I don't know if she'll ever forgive me. But I'm not going to rest until she at least gives me the chance to properly apologize for being a complete ass.

After which, it's game on.

Chapter 7

The more people I meet, the more I love my dog.

I SIGH AS I catch Ashlyn climbing through my kitchen window. She notices me sitting at my dining table watching her and waves before taking a bow. If she thinks I'm going to applaud her ability to get into my house without a key, she's sorely mistaken. What I will do is remember to lock my windows from now on.

"What are you doing here?"

"I've come to stop you from obsessing about a sexy Hollywood actor."

The nasty comment I had locked and loaded for her stalls in my mouth. I've tried everything to get my mind off Maverick Langston. Working at the Wildlife Refuge hasn't helped. Going for hikes to the falls hasn't helped. Giving the dogs flea baths hasn't helped, although even Bark Twain smells pretty now. I'm ready and willing to try another tactic.

"What's your plan?"

She squeals and does a victory dance. "I knew you'd be in."

I hold up my hand. "I'm not in yet. I want to hear your idea first. I can't spend the night in jail when my animals are dependent on me for breakfast in the morning."

She rolls her eyes. "One night. One freaking night you spent in jail. When are you going to stop throwing it in my face?"

"Never. The only reason there weren't more nights spent in jail is because we managed to get away all the other times you pulled your antics."

"Oh, please. We would have never spent the night in jail for distributing hash brownies in Winter Falls."

She's delusional. The only reason we didn't end up in jail facing a prison sentence is because the chief of police at the time ate a brownie and was too stoned to give chase. Luckily, he didn't have any recollection of dancing down Main Street in his undies the following day. Lesson learned. No helping Ashlyn out with bake sales.

"Besides, marijuana is completely legal in Colorado."

I don't bother reminding her there's a difference between a drug being legal and distributing such drug to unsuspecting people in the form of delicious, irresistible brownies. A big difference.

"What's your plan?" I repeat my question.

Her eyes light up before she announces, "We're going to solve the Mystery of the Black Hat Bandit's Missing Loot."

I groan. The Mystery of the Black Hat Bandit's Missing Loot is this wild goose chase Aspen and Ashlyn have been on to locate fifty-thousand dollars the black hat bandit, aka Robert Adams, stole from Hastings National Bank in Nebraska in

1955. They're convinced the bandit hid the money somewhere in Winter Falls for his lover, Patricia.

"Are you still going on about this? I thought you gave you up." Thought? Wished is more like it.

She rears back. "Why would I give up? Do you have me confused with someone else? I never give up. Ask Rowan if you need a reminder."

I am *not* going to ask her husband how she never gave up. There are some things about my baby sister I do not need to know.

"I thought the whole mystery was at a dead end since Ellery refuses to allow you to dig up the lawn at *The Inn on Main*."

As far as I know, the latest clue led Aspen and Ashlyn to believe the money was buried in the yard of Ellery's bed and breakfast. When Ellery heard, she lost her dang mind before putting her foot down. She's fiercely protective of the manor she shed blood and tears to renovate into a bed and breakfast. She won't let anyone damage it.

Ashlyn whistles as she suddenly finds the wall behind me fascinating. If she screamed 'I didn't listen to Ellery', it wouldn't be more obvious.

"You suck. What have you been up to?"

She shrugs. "I may have accidentally found a lockbox when I was digging in the yard of the *Inn on Main*."

I raise an eyebrow. "Accidentally?"

"I made a deal with Ellery," she says instead of answering my question.

She pauses, and I motion for her to get on with it. "What's the deal?"

Her nose wrinkles. "Ellery kept the lockbox for safekeeping."

"And you think the lockbox is full of money and you want to liberate it?"

"Unfortunately, no."

I rub my temples where I feel an Ashlyn headache coming on. "No? Then, what?"

"According to Cole, the stupid lockbox is too light to have fifty-thousand bucks in it, which means there's only one other thing the box could contain."

I'm nearly afraid to ask. "What?"

She grins. "Another clue."

Good grief. She wants me to join her on her wild goose chase. I debate telling her I'm not interested, but my phone beeps with a message. A message I have no doubt is from Mav 'can't keep my lips to myself' Langston. Distraction it is.

"And where is this lockbox at the moment?"

"In Ellery's garage. I think."

The Ashlyn headache is no longer on its way. It has arrived. "You don't know?"

"It must be. Ellery moved into her new house with Cole a week ago. With the baby coming any moment now, she hasn't had the chance to worry about the stuff in the garage. She probably forgot all about it."

I hate to agree with Ashlyn. Agreeing is encouragement in her book, but she's probably correct this time. Ellery's baby is due to arrive in less than a month. Cleaning out her garage is the last thing on her mind at the moment.

I'm going to regret this, but I motion to the door. "Let's go."

As soon as the word 'go' is out of my mouth, Bark Twain and Indiana Bones scamper to the door. They sit pretty and gaze up at me with their puppy dog eyes. I know better than to fall for those beggars' eyes.

"Sorry guys, you're staying home this time."

Indiana Bones barks while Bark Twain sprays the room with gas.

Ashlyn waves a hand in front of her face. "You need to have your dog checked out by a vet. I think there's something rotting in his intestines."

I kneel down to give Bark Twain a rub down. "There's nothing wrong with my boy. Is there?" Indiana Bones pushes his way in between us and I scratch behind his ears. "I wasn't neglecting you, my boy."

Ashlyn taps her foot. "Are we doing this today or are you going to make love to your animals first?"

"Someone's a Grumpy Gus," I whisper to my doggies before standing. "I'm ready."

We hop in a golf cart and drive in the direction of the *Inn on Main.* Before Cole bought Ellery her dream house, she lived in the carriage house behind her inn. The downstairs is a garage while her one-bedroom apartment is above.

Ashlyn parks in front of the garage and jumps out. I follow her wondering what in the world I've got myself into now. I should be back at my house burying my sorrow in a pint of chocolate chip cookie dough ice cream like a normal heartbroken woman, not galivanting around town with my baby sister who doesn't know the meaning of personal boundary.

She tries the garage door. "Dang. It's locked," she mutters before pulling a key out of her back pocket.

"Ellery gave you a key to her garage?"

"Not exactly," she admits as she opens the door.

I shackle her wrist to stop her. "If Ellery didn't give you the key, we're breaking and entering."

"It's not breaking and entering if it's family."

"I beg to differ."

"Besides, I'm the mayor now. I own this town."

Winter Falls is going to regret her volunteering to be mayor before the year is out. When Ellery was picked as the next mayor, Ashlyn couldn't scream 'I volunteer as tribute' loud enough. At the time, everyone thought it was a good idea as Ellery was still hiding her pregnancy and fighting her love of Cole. Now, we all have to live with those hasty decisions.

Ashlyn opens the door and switches on the lights. "You coming?"

Someone has to keep my baby sister in check. I walk inside and shut the door behind me. "Do you know where the lockbox is at least?"

The garage is mostly filled with garden equipment and other supplies for the inn, but it's not a mess. There are shelves and stacked containers keeping the area neat. Not a surprise since Ellery is a total workaholic. I can't wait until her baby's born and she attempts to return to work with the baby strapped on her back. Cole is going to lose his mind.

"No need. It must be there." Ashlyn points to a row of shelves and marches toward them.

I'm here. I might as well help. "What does the lockbox look like?"

"I knew you'd have fun." She elbows me. "It's rusted metal and about yay big." She indicates a box about the size of a small dog bed.

"Found it!" She picks up a box and sets it on the work bench. She curses when she tries to open it. "Damn. It's locked."

I search around the room for a tool to help us open it and find a pair of wire cutters. "Will these work?"

Ashlyn yanks the wire cutters from my hands and a slight tingle of regret travels through my mind. My baby sister is going to be the death of me.

"Worth a try."

The lock snaps open. Considering the lock's half a century old, I'm not surprised.

"Huh," Ashlyn says as she peeks into the box.

I shove her out of the way. "What is it?"

I groan when I see the piece of paper. "Another clue?" Yeah. Yeah. She said the box didn't contain the stolen money, but I still hoped.

She unfolds the paper before laying it on the table. "Almost there, my love. You'll find the item where the steel stops and families reunite," she reads the message scrawled upon the paper aloud.

Steel stops? Families reunite? "What the heck does that mean?"

"I don't know, but I'm going to figure it out."

She places the paper back in the box and shuts it before placing it on the shelf where she found it.

"Are you going to pretend we weren't here?"

"What Ellery doesn't know won't hurt her."

"What about the broken lock?"

She bats her eyelashes. "What broken lock?"

"Don't think batting your eyelashes works on me. I'm not Rowan."

"Rowan! Shit. I promised I'd be right back."

"What does your husband think you're doing?"

"Getting supplies for—"

I hold up my hand. "Nope. I don't want to hear it. I don't need to know what my sister gets up to with her husband."

She waggles her eyebrows. "Need a clue? I'm trying to get pregnant."

Gee, thanks. Another reminder of how she's found love and I never will. I whirl around and stalk out of the garage. "I'm out of here."

"You're welcome," she shouts after me.

I glance over my shoulder at her. "For what?"

"Taking your mind off he who shall not be named, of course." She winks before shutting the garage door.

"Whatever," I grump despite her being right. She did take my mind off Mav for a few minutes and I'm grateful. I am. But why can't I stop thinking about the infuriating man for more than a few minutes at a time?

Patience, Juniper. Maverick Langston doesn't belong in Winter Falls. As soon as he figures out how out of place he is, he'll skedaddle for good. Once he's gone, I can really start to forget all about him. A fist squeezes my heart at the thought, but I ignore it. My heart isn't in charge. I am.

Chapter 8

You can tell when a rabbit's in a good mood because he's hoppy.

I GLARE AT ASHLYN. "What are you talking about?"

"Legend has it Eostre mated—"

"I know the legend of the Eostre pagan festival," I growl. "What I don't know is why you're offering me an outfit for Eostre."

She beams down at me. "Because you're representing Eostre."

"We've never had anyone represent Eostre at the festival before," I point out.

"We can hardly have an Equinox without an Eostre."

I groan. I should have known. Eostre is the fertility goddess of humans and crops. According to legend, Eostre mated with the solar god of the spring, Equinox, and nine months later gave birth to a god child. The legend is the basis for our annual Eostre festival. But this festival has never included anyone playing the goddess and god before.

"It won't work, you know."

She widens her eyes in an effort to appear innocent. Innocent my ass. She's obviously concocted some plan to put me and Maverick together and I do not approve. Not one tiny bit.

"You're my baby sister. You're supposed to be on my side."

She flinches before quickly covering it up. "I'm on the side of love."

My sister being married to the man she's been in love with forever is a pain in my ass. I could remind her of all the times she didn't want to talk about Rowan when he was ignoring her, but I'm not a bitch. I am happy she's happy. What I'm not happy about is her thinking I need to be all loved up now, too.

"Don't tell me you've joined Aspen's matchmaking committee."

"There's no committee." Her eyes widen when she realizes what she said, and she slams a hand over her mouth.

"What did I do when you thought Rowan didn't want you?" Maybe I am a bit of bitch after all.

She shakes her head with her hands over her mouth.

"I'll tell you. I sat by you while you drank Long Island iced teas. I brought you movies and chocolates. I listened to you whine about the man. What didn't I do?"

When she refuses to answer, I do on her behalf. "I didn't push you into his arms."

"But—"

"And Rowan didn't do you wrong. He didn't sneak out of your bed and kiss another woman for the entire world to see."

"Maybe he accidentally kissed her?"

I raise a brow. "The same way you accidentally have a key to Ellery's garage she doesn't know about?"

She throws the pagan goddess outfit at me. "Just put it on or I'll sic the rest of our sisters on you. And you can deal with Cole for making Ellery walk all the way over here."

Another sister invasion? No, thanks. I snatch the outfit and stomp to my bedroom to get changed.

The first thing on my to-do list for Monday morning is phoning the locksmith to get my locks changed. I should probably get a security system, too. Never mind I'd literally be the only person in Winter Falls to have a security system let alone use her locks. I am done with my baby sister invading my house.

When I stroll into my living room a few minutes later, Ashlyn claps. "I knew this outfit would be perfect for you."

Apparently, her idea of perfect is my boobs threatening to fall out of the top of this dress. I raise a hand but quickly drop it again when I realize I'm about to flash her.

"Stop. I don't want to know anymore about your conniving. You got me into the outfit. Let's go."

We travel to the park north of town. The baseball field and tennis and basketball courts are crowded with townspeople gathered around for the day's festivities. Streamers from recycled paper – this is Winter Falls after all – decorate the area. There's also a stage set up in front of the bleachers at the baseball field.

Ashlyn leads me to the stage. When my gaze catches on Mav waiting there for me, I stumble on the stairs. Holy munching goats! Who picked out his outfit? He doesn't resemble a pagan god. With his naked chest and the beard he let grow out, he bears a striking resemblance to a Viking.

Vikings are always sexy, but Mav as a Viking is literally the sexiest thing I've ever seen in my life. In addition to the muscles of his chest on display, his brown trousers hug his hips and thighs. Thighs I know are strong enough to hold me up while he pounds into me.

He smirks at me and thoughts of all the scrumptious things he can do with his body to make mine sing fly out the window. Maverick Langston is not to be trusted, and I won't be forgetting it anytime soon. Unfortunately, my body doesn't get the memo and butterflies flap their wings in my stomach while my knees knock.

I lock my knees as I take my place next to him on the stage. When he reaches for my hand, I snarl at him. His eyes fill with hurt before he drops his hand. How dare he feel hurt? He's the cheater. Not me!

Ashlyn grabs the microphone. "Who's ready to party?"

I barely stop myself from rolling my eyes. My baby sister being mayor is the worst decision this town has ever made, and I was around when they thought everyone should go shoeless because of the harmful chemicals used in manufacturing shoes. Dr. Blue put a stop to the practice after several kids got infections from the cuts on their feet.

"Welcome to Winter Falls' Eostre Festival!" The crowd cheers in response. "Eostre herself is here today to open the festival. And she brought her lover, Equinox, with her."

She winks at me, and I fist my hands before I decide tugging my sister's hair out in front of the entire town is the best idea I've ever had. Will Rowan still love her if she's bald? She motions me forward.

I glare at her as I snatch the microphone from her. I force a smile on my face as I greet the crowd.

"Thank you for inviting me to your festival in my honor." I curtsy. "The egg hunt will begin from the basketball court in fifteen minutes. In the meantime, enjoy the craft fair." I motion to the booths set out on the baseball field. "Have a wonderful Eostre."

I place the microphone in the stand and hurry off the stage. Mav follows me. Of course, he does. Can he not get a hint?

"Juniper!"

I whirl around on him. "What?"

His eyes dip and flare when they land on my cleavage. I wish I could yell at him, but this outfit is practically screaming *look at my breasts!* You know it's the reason why Ashlyn picked it out.

"Ahem. Can we talk? I want to explain what happened with Quinn."

I growl at the mention of the woman he kissed when I thought we were in a relationship. Stupid me. "I think the pictures explain enough."

He steps closer, and I scoot backwards. "Please, June Bug. I'm sorry. I was an idiot. Won't you let me explain?"

"There's no time. The egg hunt is beginning."

He glances around. "Where are the children?"

I smirk. "The children's egg hunt is held at the high school. We keep the kids separated from the adults."

Trust me, it's necessary. There's too much biting and pulling of hair otherwise. And that's just how the adults act.

"But Easter eggs hunts are for kids."

"This isn't an *Easter* egg hunt." I motion toward my dress. "The pagan outfit should have been your first clue."

"At least you're gorgeous, I look like a complete tool strutting around without a shirt on. I'm afraid to sit down and rip these pants in two."

"And I can't bend over, or I'll flash the entire town." No one would mind. Clothes are optional in Winter Falls for the most part after all.

"Don't worry. I'll protect your virtue."

Ashlyn skips up to me before I can tell him I don't need him to protect me. I can protect myself. "You ready to get your ass kicked?"

"My being dressed in this ridiculous outfit is not going to stop me from winning the egg hunt."

She snorts. "When have you ever won the egg hunt? I'm the reigning champion."

"Because you're a big, fat cheater."

"You say cheater, I say smart."

"Whatever."

Once she flounces away, Mav leans close to whisper, "Is the egg hunt a contest?"

I ignore the quiver of excitement that runs through my body at the feel of his breath on my skin. "You bet it is. Whoever collects the most eggs wins dinner at the brewery for two." I shake my finger at him. "Don't be getting any ideas. I'm going to finally win this year."

"Maybe we could work together."

I should know better, but I ask anyway, "What do you have in mind?"

He winks. "You gather the eggs. I got this."

I shrug. "Whatever."

Forest blows a whistle. "One minute."

Mav kisses my forehead. "Off I go."

While I watch his ass as he saunters away, I can feel my skin tingle where his lips touched it. Sigh. Too bad he's not to be trusted because his lips and that ass… I push those thoughts out of my mind. *Now's not the time to reminisce about biting those juicy muscles, Juniper.* It's time to finally beat Ashlyn in the egg hunt.

Forest begins the countdown. "Five, four, three, two, one!"

At one, everyone rushes off. I lift up my skirts and realize this outfit isn't so bad after all. You're not allowed to carry a basket during the egg hunt. Not after one too many people ended up getting bashed over the head with one. My skirt is the perfect place to gather my eggs. This is my year to win. Mine!

While the rest of the participants scurry around the basketball area, I make my way to the tennis court. I gather up several eggs before anyone joins me. I search the area for signs of my sister and notice Mav whispering to her. I don't know what they're whispering about, but I do know she's not gathering eggs. Go, Mav!

After five minutes my skirt is weighed down with green, yellow, and purple eggs – the colors representing Oestre. I carefully make my way to the counting station where everyone places their eggs. I notice the other piles and how small they are. Yes! There's no need to count this year. I'm clearly the winner.

Mav joins me. "I guess we'll be going out for a dinner at the brewery."

I narrow my eyes at him. "Who said you'd be joining me?"

His eyes flash with hurt. Damn. I've become a shrew.

"I'm—"

Before I have the chance to apologize, the other participants join us. Love Hill sidles up to Mav.

"Hi, handsome," she breathes out. My nostrils flare as I glare at her. Love Hill is a hussy who chases after all the men. Ask me sometime about how she tried to ruin Aspen and Lyric's relationship.

"How you doing, sweetheart?" Mav responds and flashes her his Hollywood smile.

My mouth snaps shut. Was I seriously going to apologize for the hurt I caused him? Ha! No need for apologizing. Maverick is the same player he's been all along. I had a temporary lapse of judgment due to his shirtless situation is all. I won't have another one.

Chapter 9

Of course, you fail. You're only human. You're not a dog.

MAVERICK

I flash my Hollywood smile at the high school secretary. "Hi, I'm here to see Principal West."

She frowns at me. "Do you have an appointment?"

"Yes," I lie and feel my cheeks begin to ache from my forced smile.

She studies the schedule in front of her. "What's your name?"

"Um. Maverick."

"Last name," she barks.

"Langston."

She hums as she flips through the schedule. "I don't have any appointment for Maverick Langston in Principal West's calendar."

Maverick Langston? Does she seriously not know who I am? This doesn't happen in Hollywood, let alone a small town in Colorado.

"Sweetheart," I begin.

She waves away my attempt at charming her. "I don't care if you are some big shot actor in Hollywood. Here in Winter

Falls, everyone is equal. Don't think I'll be doing you any favors because you're a bigwig celebrity, because I won't."

I guess she knows who I am after all. Unfortunately, she's not impressed. And honestly, why should she be? As she says, everyone is equal. Have I been pushing myself on the residents of Winter Falls because I'm famous? Am I the asshole Juniper says I am?

I need to think about how I interact with the town but now is not the time. Not when I'm on a mission to get Juniper's mom on my side in the 'make Juniper give Maverick a chance' battle.

"Can you ring Mrs. West and ask if she has a moment for me?"

She purses her lips at me. "What's this regarding?"

"Um…" I'm not exactly fired up to spill my guts to Juniper's mom. Making even more of a fool out of myself in front of a woman I don't know is not on my agenda.

She ducks her head but not before I notice her mouth curve.

"Never mind." She picks up the phone. "I know what you're here for."

I cringe. She does? Does the entire town know about me and Juniper? About how I'm chasing a woman who seems to want nothing to do with me? No need to worry about making a fool out of myself any longer. Mission accomplished.

She speaks for a moment on the phone before setting it down. "You can go in." She gestures toward an office behind her.

"Thank you."

She snorts. "Don't thank me."

I get not being impressed by my Hollywood credentials, but good manners are good manners. Why wouldn't I thank her?

I knock on the open office door before peeking inside. "Mrs. West?"

"Good. You're here." She stands. "Follow me."

"Were you expecting me?"

She smiles and I'm reminded of Juniper's smile. Other than the smile, the mother and daughter appear nothing alike. Mrs. West is tiny with blonde hair and blue eyes, whereas Juniper is two inches shorter than my height of five-foot-eight, has dark hair, and those green eyes I want to drown in.

Mrs. West laughs. "I knew you'd stop by at some point. And, please, call me Ruby."

"Where are we going, Ruby?" I ask as I hurry through the halls of the school after her.

"I figured you wouldn't mind helping me out." She winks.

"Of course not."

She knocks on a door marked custodian. When no one answers, she enters. I fidget in the hallway trying to figure out if I'm supposed to follow her or not. She returns before I can make up my mind. She's holding some contraption I'm not familiar with. I wouldn't dare say what it does.

"Let me carry that for you." I relieve her of the equipment before she can protest.

"Such a gentleman." She pats my arm. Good thing she doesn't know about the things I've done with her daughter. She winks up at me. "And, yes, I know you've had sexual relations with my daughter."

I choke on air. "What? How do you know?"

"A mother always knows," she sings. "I'll have a package of condoms delivered to your house later today."

I trip and nearly end up on my ass before righting myself. "I can handle protection."

She stops and studies me for a moment before nodding. "Okay, I'm trusting you to use the appropriate prophylactics while courting my daughter. After the courtship is over, though." She grins. "I can't wait to be a grandmother. Another grandchild would be a blessing."

I haven't managed to convince Juniper to allow me to properly apologize and her mom is talking about me getting her pregnant and giving her grandchildren. Have I landed on *Fantasy Island?*

"Don't worry about Juniper. She's stubborn. All my girls are." And she couldn't seem prouder. A bell rings, and she consults her watch. "We don't have much time. Let's go."

I have no idea where we're going, but I follow her out of the school and along a path until we reach a football field.

I whistle as I scan the area. The football field is surrounded by a track. Next to which are bleachers. The set-up is impressive. I didn't expect a small town to have this nice of sports facilities.

"Rowan Hansley donated the money to improve the football field and track," Ruby explains as we walk across the track and onto the football field. "You must have met him. He's married to my youngest daughter, Ashlyn."

"We've met." I don't tell her we met in a bar when the three men attached to her daughters decided to give me the third degree.

"Okay. This is a lining machine, and this is how it works." She takes the equipment from me and angles it toward a faded line on the field before pushing a button and white paint shoots out. After her quick demonstration, she gives the equipment back to me. "Soccer season is starting soon, and the lines need to be adjusted from football to soccer."

"Okay," I say; unsure of what's happening here.

She indicates the sticks and twine set up throughout the field. "Follow the twine and you'll be fine." She waits until I nod. "Thanks again," she shouts as she walks off.

I search the field for a clue as to what just happened. Did she enlist my help without actually asking me? Mrs. West is sneaky. I think we're going to get along fine.

I study the twine and decide to begin in the corner. I don't make it to the other side of the field before sweat is dripping off my brow. I lay the lining machine on its side before whipping my t-shirt off. Cheers erupt.

I glance over at the bleachers to discover the gossip gals clapping from the stands. Next to them sits Juniper's sisters. They wave at me.

"How did you know I was here?" I yell my question.

Aspen gestures toward her mom's secretary. "Welcome to small town living."

Rowan appears from behind the bleachers. Ashlyn catcalls him and he waves at her. "Be good, dream girl."

"You enjoy it when I'm bad! A lot!"

He smirks as he approaches me. "She's not wrong." He offers me a sports bottle.

"What's in this?" I ask but don't hesitate to chug the liquid.

"Don't worry. Unlike some people, I won't drug you."

I spit out the drink. "What?"

He pats me on the back. "I told you *not* to worry."

"You also mentioned people drugging me."

He shrugs. "Not drugging as in killing you. More like drugging you so you can have a good time."

I hold up my hand. "Say no more. I don't want to know."

"Mrs. West put you to work, did she?"

"I came here to talk to her about how to figure out a way to win over her daughter and she gave me this lining thing and left me here."

"You best get to work. Ruby is a hard ass."

I motion to the bleachers. "What's going on with them?"

"They're here to watch the show. What else would they be doing?"

"What show?"

"Dude, you took off your shirt. You are the show."

I puff up my chest. I work hard to keep my body toned. I don't mind showing it off, although it does feel a bit creepy how everyone's watching me work while – I squint at them – eating snacks and drinking beer.

"Are they drinking beer at a high school?"

Rowan growls. "Ashlyn better not be drinking."

He tries to march off, but I step in front of him. He may be nearly a foot taller than me and have a good fifty pounds on me, but I am not letting him dictate to his wife.

"And you better not be dictating what your wife can and cannot drink."

He claps me on the shoulder. "We're trying to get pregnant."

"Ah." I step out of his way.

"And we're having a ball."

"Nope. I don't want to hear about Juniper's baby sister's sex life."

"She's not my sister." He smirks before sauntering off.

Ashlyn screeches before sprinting away and he gives chase. I chuckle before picking up the lining machine and getting back to work. When I reach the corner and turn around, I notice the crowd has grown. I scan the people but there's no Juniper.

Damn. I know Juniper still wants me – she can't hide the way her eyes flare or her cheeks darken whenever her gaze lands on my chest – and I'm not above using her physical attraction to me to reel her in. This unexpected job is the perfect opportunity to show off for her, but she's apparently avoiding me. Good thing she can't avoid me forever.

Chapter 10

Dolphins are beyond smart. Within weeks of captivity, they can train people to stand on the edge of a pool and throw them fish.

I TRUDGE UP THE stairs to my parents' house. It's Sunday aka family dinner time. Don't get me wrong, I'm not a curmudgeon. I love my family, and I want to spend time with them. But I'm also not oblivious to what's happening in town as in a certain man running around trying to get my attention, which means the main topic of discussion today will be the one and only Maverick Langston.

Save me. I never want to hear his name again. Stupid flirty man who can't keep his smiles or lips to himself.

I fling the door open. "I'm—" My greeting dies in my throat when I notice who has joined us for family dinner.

"You're what?" Lilac asks.

I ignore her question to march over to Mav who's standing in the living room with Rowan and Cole as if nothing's wrong – as if he's welcome here. I think not. "Who do you think you are?"

"Wait. You know he's Maverick Langston, don't you? Isn't he your secret admirer?" Lilac wouldn't understand a rhetorical question if one bit her in the ass.

"Not so secret anymore," Ashlyn sings. "Although, I always knew."

I can feel my nostrils flare as I shoot daggers out of my eyes at her. "Being a peeping Tom is illegal. The police should arrest you. Where's Lyric?"

The door opens and the Chief of Police walks in. "I'm here. What did I miss?"

Aspen kisses his cheek before informing him, "Juniper's losing her mind."

"You know it's not actually possible to lose your mind. To be lost means—"

I shove my palm in Lilac's face. "Enough with the lectures. You know exactly what she meant."

Here's the thing about Lilac. She takes everything literally, but she does understand the figurative meaning. She's just determined to use any excuse she can to lecture us about proper English grammar. I don't know why. The woman is an environmental engineer, not an English teacher. She's supposed to be saving the earth, not delivering lectures about the literal meaning of expressions.

"She's going to blow," Ashlyn whisper-shouts.

The door opens behind Lyric, and Ellery waddles in. "You better not be talking about me and this baby."

Cole leads Ellery to the sofa and helps her settle. She groans as she puts her feet on the coffee table. "Can someone check if my shoes match? I haven't seen my feet in months."

Cole sighs. "Ellie girl, you don't think I'd purposely dress you in two different shoes, do you?"

"No, but I also thought – wrongly as it turns out – you knew the difference between navy blue and black."

"It was dark. I didn't notice."

The sliding door to the dining room opens, and Mom bounces inside with Dad following her. "Oh good. Everyone's here."

"Um, Ruby." Rowan points to her hair where a leaf is sticking out.

"Oops!" Mom pulls the leaf out before winking up at Dad.

Ashlyn covers her face with her hands. "Someone save me."

"Why must you persist in these theatrics about our parents' sex life? You know they have sex. How do you think you came into existence?"

Ashlyn feigns gagging at Lilac's pronouncement. "Stop. I'm begging you – stop."

"I don't care about Mom and Dad having sex. I want to know what Mav is doing here."

Mom shrugs at my pronouncement. "I invited him."

I swear I can feel the top of my head nearing explosion. I always thought those emojis with someone's head blowing off were an exaggeration. They're not. "Why? Why would you invite him?"

"I've never had a famous person to dinner before."

"Hey!" Ashlyn huffs. "Rowan's famous."

Mom ignores her. "Besides, he's your secret admirer. Why wouldn't I invite him?"

I throw my hands in the air. "Maybe because he stuck his tongue down another woman's throat when we were dating."

Mav clears his throat. "No tongue was involved."

"You have got to be kidding me!" I screech. Yes, screech. My annoyance has reached the danger levels. "You're quibbling over how deep the kiss was?"

"If you'd let me explain…"

I am done with this. He wants to explain? I'll let him and once he's fallen into the hole he's dug, we'll be done with this stupid song and dance routine we've got going on.

I cross my arms over my chest and lift my chin. "Go ahead. Explain to everyone how you thought it was okay to kiss another woman the day after you left me in your bed."

"Can I record this?" Ashlyn asks with her phone already aimed at Mav.

"Dream girl." Rowan nabs the phone from her. "Privacy."

Ashlyn sticks out her bottom lip. "But imagine the kind of cash I could make from selling the video."

"Because you don't make enough money narrating erotic romances and owning a recording studio?" She shrugs at her husband's question. "What about being married to a million-aire?"

Her shoulders slump. "Oh, yeah. I forgot." She nods to Mav. "Go ahead. I won't record."

"Quinn Wilder means nothing to me."

I roll my eyes. "Which is why you were kissing her for the entire world to see."

"It was a publicity stunt."

A publicity stunt? "You kissed someone in public and let the world believe you're involved with her for publicity?" I seethe.

His cheeks darken and I do not pay attention to how adorable he is when he blushes. Nope. Not I.

He shrugs. "It's part of the whole Hollywood gig. The producer of my latest project wanted to create more interest in the film. Her idea was to make it appear as if the two lead actors fell in love during the filming."

"It worked," Ashlyn says, and I growl at her. "Don't shoot the messenger. I can't change the facts." She wiggles her phone at me. "The box office revenue the weekend after the incident was twice the weekend before."

"Let me get this straight." I pause to gather my thoughts. "You kissed another woman in public to make it appear as if you're in a relationship with her when you were supposed to be in a relationship with me because it helped increase the box office revenue?"

Mav's shoulders hunch forward. "I feel like this is a trick question."

Rowan sighs. "Because it is, dude. It is."

"Can I decline to answer?"

"There's no reason to answer," I tell him. "You've said enough."

"Out of curiosity what exactly did I say?"

I sum it up for him because I want this done once and for all. Also, men are idiots. You can't assume they understand their own idiocy.

"You said I'm not as important as making a boatload of money. You said my feelings were immaterial. You said what we had wasn't important to you. You said our relationship was worth throwing away for money."

He blanches and gulps a few times before speaking, "I didn't say any of those things."

I cross my arms over my chest. "Yeah, you did." I motion to my sisters. "Ask any woman in here."

Ashlyn, Aspen, and Lilac move to stand behind me. Ellery waves from the couch. "I'm metaphorically standing behind my sister. Pretend I can actually stand."

"Shit," he swears. "How do I fix this?"

I raise an eyebrow at him. "How can I ever trust you to not do the exact same thing again but with another woman?"

"Publicity stunts are part of the Hollywood life."

His words feel like knives slicing into me; leaving my heart bloody and bruised. I knew he was a Hollywood star the first time he talked his way into my pants, but I – stupidly as it turns out – thought he was genuinely interested in me. Instead, he was playing me.

And he's still trying to play me. Good luck. I know better now. This girl is done being played.

"Thanks for dinner, Mom." I kiss her on the cheek. "I'm not feeling well. I'm going home."

"Baby girl," she mutters in response, but I hold up my hand before she can continue. I'm not interested in her platitudes about life always working out at this moment.

"Do you want me to kick his ass?" Dad asks and despite feeling as if my heart is being torn in two, I manage a smile for him.

"I think they'll kick you out of the hippie club."

Dad may be a stone cold lawyer, but he's a hippie and a member of the non-violent club first and foremost.

"They won't kick me out," Lyric announces before snapping his fingers at Mav. "You. I think you've worn out your welcome."

Mav raises his hands in surrender. "I can see myself out."

"You don't need to—" Mom starts, but Dad cuts her off.

"Yes, he does."

Everyone watches as Mav saunters out of the house and shuts the door behind him.

Aspen winks at me. "We've got your back."

I hope this means they'll stop trying to matchmake me, but I won't hold my breath. Aspen is on a mission to ensure all of her sisters are blissfully in love. Sorry, Aspen, not going to happen.

"Shall we eat?" Mom asks after an awkward silence falls.

"I'm not hungry," I declare before making my way to the front door. "I should check on my animals anyway."

I scurry out of the house as fast as I can. I don't want to witness the pity on everyone's faces. My love story is the same as theirs. Mine doesn't end in an engagement ring or baby. No, mine ends in heartache.

I check which way Mav is walking before hopping on my bike and pedaling in the opposite direction. I rub my chest as I think of him abandoning Winter Falls and never coming back. Damn it. I won't miss him. I refuse to miss the man who made it crystal clear where I stand on his priority list. Hint. It's not very high.

Chapter 11

There's one surefire way to catch a squirrel. Climb a tree and act like a nut.

I RUSH INTO THE hospital with Rowan and Ashlyn. In front of us are my parents. Behind us are Aspen and Lyric and Lilac. It's a West family invasion.

"Where do we go?" I ask as I search the area.

"This way." Aspen motions toward the elevator. "Sage said the maternity ward is on the third floor."

"I don't understand how Sage got here before us," I complain. "We're the baby's actual aunts."

Rowan snorts. "If you don't think the gossip gals have been scouting Ellery and Cole's house for the past week, you're sorely mistaken."

My irritation dies a quick death. He's not wrong. Naturally, the gossip gals have been camped outside of Ellery's house waiting for the arrival of the baby. The small population of Winter Falls combined with the mostly aging residents means there aren't many babies born. The arrival of Ellery and Cole's child is a big deal. Not to mention the amount of betting surrounding the event has reached epic proportions.

Before the elevator doors even open, I hear Feather complaining, "I know Ellery West is here. I don't give a toot about your stupid hip rules."

"I should explain to her what HIPAA means," Lilac mutters.

We exit the elevator to discover Feather, Petal, Sage, Cayenne, and Clove facing off with a nurse.

Cole steps out of a room, and Feather screeches, "There he is," before charging toward him. "Where's the baby? How is he? Is it a he? What did you name him?"

"Ellery's fine by the way," Ellery hollers from her room.

The gossip gals try to push past Cole, but he blocks them. "I'm sorry ladies. You're going to have to wait in the reception area."

"What about me? Do I have to stay in the reception area, too?" Mom asks before engulfing Cole in a hug. "Don't worry. Daniel will escort them to the waiting room."

Cole scans the area and gulps when he notices the crowd that's gathered.

"Is the entire town of Winter Falls here?" he asks.

"No, just the gossip gals and West family," Lilac answers.

Aspen elbows her. "He was being ironic."

"I don't think you understand the term ironic."

Ellery screams, and Cole races into their hospital room without a backward glance.

"Come on," Mom says and waves toward the waiting room.

I have no problem following her command. Unlike the gossip gals, I have no interest in observing the birth of my niece. I've seen enough animals born. I have no desire to watch my sister bear a child. I would never be able to scrub those memories from my mind. No thanks.

I stroll into the waiting room but skid to a stop when I notice the man who's already sitting in one of the chairs.

"What are you doing here?" I yell at Mav.

Mom squirms next to me, and I snarl at her. "What did you do?"

"I invited him. He's family."

My eyebrows nearly fly off my forehead. "Family? Have you lost your mind? Have the high school kids finally driven you around the bend? Has too much sex with Dad caused you to lose all your brain cells?"

"Sex actually grows more brain cells," Lilac explains. "Consistent sex generates brain cells in the area of the hippocampus. The hippocampus region is associated with information retention."

"Can someone kill her for me?" I ask the ceiling.

"I've asked you not to discuss killing your siblings in front of me," Lyric mumbles before he grasps Lilac's elbow and leads her out of the room.

"Why are you leading me away? I'm not the one threatening to commit sororicide," I hear Lilac say, but I ignore her. She's Lyric's problem now.

I aim my daggers at Mom. "I'm being serious, Mom. Mav is not part of the family."

"You should talk to him."

I close my eyes and inhale a deep breath. Committing matricide at the hospital is a bad idea. I love my mom. I do. I don't truly want to kill her, although it's hard to remember why not at the moment. Besides, who would tend to my animals while I'm in prison?

"I'm sorry, June Bug. I didn't mean to intrude."

At Mav's apology, my gaze lands on him. I scowl at him, but he appears genuinely upset. Am I being a bitch? I study the people in the room, but no one will meet my gaze. Yep. It's confirmed. I'm a bitch.

"Let's go," I tell him and whirl around to march out of the room.

I don't glance back, but I can hear him following me. We climb into the elevator.

"Can I—"

I shake my head. "Not yet." He nods.

We exit the elevator, then the building, but I don't stop. Not yet. We may not be in Winter Falls, but there are spies everywhere. I finally stop at the opposite end of the parking lot.

"What are you doing here?"

"Your mom messaged me to let me know Ellery's having her baby. I didn't think. I jumped in my car and rushed over here. I thought you might need me."

He didn't think. He thought I needed him and boom! He came here. My tummy warms at the idea. Damn. I hate how easily he can bring a response from my body.

"I'm sorry I was a bitch up there."

"I understand. After you explained how," he cringes. "the kiss made you feel, I can't blame you."

Good. At least, we understand each other now. Moving on.

"When are you leaving town?"

His brow wrinkles. "Leaving town? Why would I leave town?"

Because leaving is what he does best. He flits into town, we have a few wonderful days and I start to believe our relationship is going places, before – boom! – he's off to greener pastures and I don't hear from him for weeks.

I cross my arms over my chest. "When?"

"June Bug," he whispers and reaches for me. I step back and his arm falls. "I deserve your anger."

Gee. Ya think? I think he deserves an ass whopping but beating the hell out of your boss is frowned upon even when said boss deserves it and then there's the whole thing about Winter Falls being non-violent.

"I'm not going anywhere until you give me a second chance."

I raise an eyebrow. "So you can leave me high and dry again?"

"I didn't mean…" His words fall off, and he shakes his head. "I need to earn your trust again."

He does, but I have no idea how he could ever earn my trust back after proving to me a publicity stunt is more important than us.

"Have you guys made up yet?" Ashlyn shouts her question from across the parking lot.

"What do you think?"

"I think Ellery's about to have her baby and the pot is up to five thousand dollars."

What am I doing? I shouldn't be fighting with Mav – no matter how big of a jerk he is – in a hospital parking lot. I should be inside the hospital waiting on the birth of my niece or nephew.

"Go," Mav says, and I focus my concentration on him. He reaches forward and squeezes my hand before I can shake him off. "We'll talk more later."

"Okay," I mumble, although I don't know what more there is to talk about.

I watch him saunter to his car and peel out of the parking lot. How he thought he was hiding in Winter Falls while driving a Maserati is beyond me.

Ashlyn threads her arm through my elbow. "When I left, Ellery was screaming up a storm at Cole. The baby's arrival should be imminent." Her smile dims, and I pat her hand.

"It's your turn next."

She frowns. "Project Get Ashlyn Pregnant has been a bust thus far."

"You have time. You only got married a few months ago after a courtship of barely a month."

She clears her throat before skipping toward the elevators. "Today is about Ellery."

A few minutes after we return to the waiting room, Cole wanders into the room carrying a squirming bundle. He appears shell-shocked, but happiness is beaming from him.

"I'd like to introduce you to Willow Amy Hawkins." Before the words are out of his mouth, he's surrounded by everyone.

"West-Hawkins," Ellery shouts from her hospital bed.

"Let me hold my grandchild," Mom insists, but she doesn't wait for Cole to relinquish his baby girl. She takes him. "Hi, Willow. I'm your grandma."

She sniffles and Dad wraps an arm around her. "And I'm your grandad."

"Here's your winnings." Sage holds out a wad of cash.

I blink at the money. "You brought the pot to the hospital?"

She waves the money and I grab it. "I don't know how you knew the baby would be named Willow."

I smirk as I stash the cash in my pocket. "I know my sister," is all I say.

I don't mention how Aspen was named after the tree in the yard of the apartment building Mom and Dad were living in when Aspen was born and how there's a willow tree on the lawn of Ellery's bed and breakfast. It's better to keep information flow to the gossip gals limited.

"Are you ready to meet your Aunt Juniper?" Mom coos at the baby before laying Willow into my waiting arms.

I sniff and new baby smell fills my nostrils. Nothing can compare to it. It's even better than puppy breath, which says it all in my opinion. I want this. I want a baby. One who has Mav's blue eyes and high cheekbones.

I clear my throat before I can start to blubber like a baby. It's not healthy to want things you can't have. And I can't have

Maverick Langston no matter how much he begs. The man is not to be trusted.

Chapter 12

I bought a dog from a blacksmith. When I got him home, he made a bolt for the door.

I'm dragging as I lay my bike against the fence at the Wildlife Refuge a week later. I haven't slept well since Mav rolled into town, but after confronting him at the hospital and being reminded of everything I can never have, sleep has disappeared. I can barely remember how well-rested feels.

I groan when I scan the area and notice Mav's car in the parking lot. What now? Do I not deserve a clean break?

As much as I'd prefer to turn around and pedal my butt on home, I better go figure out what he's up to. After the last time he visited, it took me forever to settle the capybaras. Although, I'll accept the extra work any day of the week to watch Mav fall into their swimming pool and flail around in fear of being bitten by the rodents who are, for the most part, harmless. Now there's a video someone would pay a ton of money for.

I open the gates of the refuge and go in search of Mav. He's not in the miniature pig enclosure. He isn't goofing around with the llamas. I don't bother checking the capybara area. I think he learned his lesson there.

I'm surprised to discover him in the fennec fox fenced-in area. If you aren't familiar with fennec foxes, let me tell you, they are the cutest fox in existence. They have these adorable oversized pointy ears, bushy tails, and they're fluffy. It's no wonder people think they'll make a good pet.

Spoiler alert – no exotic animals make good pets. Fennec foxes act as if they've just shot five espressos. Seriously. Their energy levels are out of this world. Also, they can never be truly potty trained and need companionship.

Despite the warnings, Hollywood stars buy the foxes for their children as if they aren't wild animals in need of specialized care. When the parents realize the care required or – more probable – when the fox eats one of their Bentley sofas, the poor fox gets shipped off to me at the Wildlife Refuge.

"What are you doing?" I holler to Mav.

He stands and twirls around. "I'm replenishing their water supply." He holds up a water bottle.

Dang. I can't be mean to him when he's being helpful.

"I meant, what are you doing here?" Apparently, I lied. I can be mean.

"I'm helping you out. I didn't realize how much work it is for you to care for these animals every day."

Helping me out? He disappears for days and re-fills one water tray and suddenly he's Mr. Helpful? Sell it to another woman 'cuz I ain't buying.

I fist my hands on my hips. "And now you do realize how much work it is?"

I wouldn't call it work. For me, caring for these animals is a labor of love. Animals are easy. You give them food, water, and attention, and they love you forever. Humans? You can give them all the attention in the world, and they still won't love you in the morning.

"I've spent the past week learning how to care for the animals here in the refuge."

He has? I raise an eyebrow. "What did you do? Watch YouTube videos?"

I don't care what the rest of the world thinks. You cannot learn everything on the Internet. There are some jobs you need to attend actual college classes for. No video can replace class lectures and studying in my opinion.

"I spent a week shadowing Dr. Skinner."

My eyes widen in surprise. Dr. Skinner is the wildlife veterinarian connected to the refuge.

"He asked how you are. Multiple times in fact. He likes you."

I roll my eyes. "Of course, he likes me. The Wildlife Refuge is his biggest client."

Mav snorts. "No, he likes you as in he wants you. I bet he's asked you out." I glance away, and he growls. "Have you dated?"

Oh no, he didn't. "Are you accusing me of dating someone? Where do you get off? I'm not the one who kissed other people while we were supposedly in a relationship."

"There's no supposedly about it. We were in a relationship."

"Did Quinn Wilder know you were in a relationship?"

He rears back as if I slapped him, but I don't want to talk about 'us' – there is no us – or his transgression.

"I've never dated Dr. Skinner. His past doesn't exactly instill confidence. He's on divorce number three."

Mav's shoulders slump in relief and I realize I should have kept my big mouth shut. Idiot. We need to move on. While standing in an enclosure with a dozen fennec foxes is not the time to re-hash the past.

"So, what? You're going to come out here and help me every day? Let me guess. You'll keep coming around until I agree to give you a second chance."

In which case, he'll be coming around forever.

"Or until you agree to go out on a date with me."

"A date? As in we'll order take-out and watch television on your sofa?"

This is what we always end up doing and it doesn't exactly spell date. Not when the man is used to wining and dining at the best eating establishments Hollywood and LA have to offer.

"Nope. I'm taking you out to a restaurant."

"In public?"

His brow wrinkles. "Yes, in public. Restaurants are public places after all."

"But you don't want to be seen out with me."

"Do you think I'm ashamed of you?"

Of course, I do. He's never wanted to be seen in public with me before. What am I supposed to think? Except that I'm his dirty little secret. The woman he's too embarrassed to escort in public because she's a hick who spends her days cleaning animal crap.

"June Bug," he growls his nickname for me, and butterflies explode in my stomach. I rub a hand over my middle. *Knock it off. He's still the man who cheated on us.* The butterflies don't seem to care as they flap their wings.

"I'm not ashamed of you."

I snort. "Whatever. We need to get to work."

"What's it going to take for me to convince you to go on a date with me?"

Hell freezing over.

When I don't respond, he pushes. "What about if we make a wager? If I win, I have the privilege of escorting you to dinner. We can go to the brewery with the dinner we won for the egg hunt at the Eostre festival."

"We won? I'm fairly certain I was the one who used the skirt on my ridiculous outfit to gather the eggs."

"We were a team. I kept Ashlyn too occupied to hunt eggs, remember?"

I do remember. I remember the two of them whispering together. "What were you talking about with my baby sister?"

He smirks. "Sorry, top secret. Restricted to need to know."

Whatever. They can have their secrets. I don't care. Besides, Ashlyn can't keep a secret to save her life.

"What do you want to wager on?"

He opens his arms wide. "Ask me anything about the Wildlife Refuge. If I can't come up with the answer, you win."

I tap my toe. "How about if I ask you to perform a few tasks?"

And I know just the perfect task.

"Go for it."

I open my mouth to respond, but he stops me.

"Do you agree to the terms of the bet?"

"What do I get if I win?"

"Anything you want."

Anything I want? Challenge accepted. "What if I want your Maserati?"

He shrugs. "If you win, we'll find a notary to sign the title over to you."

"My dad's a notary," I tell him and reach out my hand.

His warm hand engulfs mine and a spark of awareness shoots from my hand through my arm and down to my belly where those stupid butterflies flap their wings with everything they've got in response. I yank my hand away before the temptation to pull him near – to hell with the consequences and broken heart – becomes too much.

Mav stares at me with heat in his eyes and I retreat a step. *Jumping him is a bad idea, Juniper.* Remember Quinn and publicity stunts and how he's not to be trusted.

I nod to the fennec fox enclosure. "I need you to weigh the foxes and fill out the diary. After which, you need to check their urine and stool."

Instead of balking at the words urine and stool, he nods and asks, "Where are the diary and scale?"

"I'll bring them," I say and hurry to get the items before I can melt into him. There's nothing sexier than a man willing to check animal urine samples in my book. I don't care how weird the idea makes me sound.

By the time I return to the fox enclosure with the diary and scale, Mav is cuddling several of the foxes. Dang. I guess the foxes are more susceptible to his charm than the capybaras.

Mav makes quick work of weighing the animals and recording the information in the diary. My hands shake as I retrieve the items from him. Is he going to win this bet? I can't back out of a bet. The people of Winter Falls would banish me if they found out. Dang it!

I nod to the hay on the ground. "Have you checked their urine and stool yet?"

He grins before kneeling on the ground. To his credit, he doesn't cover his mouth and nose when he finds a pile of stool. Considering how bad it smells, I can't help but admire him.

"Stool appears good."

I decide this is now a teaching moment. "What are you checking for?"

"Too fatty or too much veg in the stool."

When I keep my mouth shut, he winks up at me. "Didn't expect me to know the answer, did you?"

No, I didn't, but I ask him to check the urine instead.

He frowns. "I think there might be urine crystals."

Shit. This is no game. I kneel next to him. "Those are indeed urine crystals. What do we do?"

"Dr. Skinner suggested using cranberry extract. I believe I saw a bottle in the supply cabinet."

I sigh as I stand. "I guess you win."

Mav glances up at me. I expect him to be smirking, but he's not. His eyes are full of hope. "No more questions? I'm up to the challenge."

"I'll get the cranberry extract," I answer and stomp away.

Shit. Shit. Shit. Now I have to go out on a date with Mav. In public. Where everyone can observe us. Dammit. I need to learn not to accept every bet thrown my way. And those butterflies in my stomach doing a happy dance need to cut it out. This date means nothing. Judging by their inability to stop dancing, they don't believe me.

Love a duck. Disaster and heartbreak here I come.

Chapter 13

If an animal's eyes have the power to speak a great language, I don't want to know what those beady chipmunk eyes are trying to tell me.

MAVERICK

I shift my weight from foot to foot before I raise my hand to knock on Juniper's door for our date. I wanted to bring the Maserati to show off for her, but cars are not allowed in the environmentally conscious Winter Falls. So, instead, I'm rocking grandpa's golf cart. I don't think she's impressed with material items anyway – despite claiming to want to win my luxury car in our bet. No, she was trying to hit me where it hurts.

She has no idea how little I care for the cars and houses and other trappings of wealth associated with being a star. None of it means a thing if I don't have her by my side. These past months when she refused to talk to me, I came to some harsh realities.

Starting with how all of it feels empty without Juniper by my side. I took her for granted. I assumed she'd always be waiting here for me no matter what. I learned the hard way how untrue my assumptions were.

And now I have to win her back. I don't care what I have to do. I will weasel my way back into her life and her heart, because Juniper's mine.

The door opens, and a dog flies out. He's followed by another dog and a – is that a chipmunk?

"Stop Dale!" Juniper shouts. Dale has to be the chipmunk, right?

I chase after him and he dashes up a tree. Shit. What now? I ditch my leather loafers and begin climbing the tree. He peers over at me from the end of a low branch. Is he laughing at me?

"If I rattle the branch, can you catch him?" I ask Juniper. When she doesn't answer, I glance over my shoulder to discover her staring at my backside. I wiggle my ass and watch her eyes widen. The weaseling my way back into Juniper's life has begun.

"June Bug!"

She startles and a blush spreads across her cheeks and down her neck to the top of her shirt. I know from experience the blush will continue to her breasts. My pants tighten. Uh oh. Wrapped around a tree trying to save a chipmunk is not the appropriate time to get hard.

"I got him," she hollers.

I jiggle the branch and the chipmunk loses his smile. Ha! That's what you get for laughing at my tree climbing capabilities. Great. I'm having a conversation in my head with a chipmunk.

As I watch, the animal falls and Juniper catches him. She immediately cuddles him like he's a baby and not an annoying rodent. The woman does love her animals.

"Back in the house with you," she coos to him, "or I won't let your brother Chip come over tomorrow for a play date."

I climb down the tree and slip my shoes back on. When Juniper notices me brushing off my slacks, she cringes.

"Sorry, Mav. I'll have those dry cleaned for you. I know how important your clothes are to you."

Whoa. Does she think I'm some materialistic man who's obsessed with the trappings of wealth? I glance down at my Prada loafers and wince. What was I thinking putting on Prada loafers and Versace khakis to accompany Juniper to the local brewery? I was thinking she'd be impressed. She's obviously not.

"It's fine. These are old anyway." I hold my breath and hope she buys my lie.

"Okay." She doesn't appear to believe me, but as long as she doesn't call me on my lie, we're good. "Let me round up Bark Twain and Indiana Bones and we can go."

"Do you want me to search for them?"

"I got this," she murmurs before clearing her throat and yelling at the top of her lungs. "Bark Twain! Indiana Bones! Get your furry butts home or you will not be getting a cheese treat ever again. Cheese!"

I hear barking before the two dogs blast out of the next door neighbor's hedge and barrel to the door. They screech to a halt at Juniper's feet and stare up at her with their puppy dog eyes.

She immediately melts, and suddenly I'm jealous of two furry mutts. Why can't she melt for me the way she does her dogs?

She places Dale on her shoulder before digging two treats out of her pockets for the dogs. They snap them up and she motions inside her house. "Get moving."

They scurry inside, and she turns to me. "I'm ready to go now."

"Were you planning to bring a chipmunk with you?" I wave toward her shoulder. "I'm fine with it, but I don't know if they'll serve him at the brewery."

She rolls her eyes before picking Dale up and setting him down in her hallway and shutting the door behind her.

"There! Now, I'm ready."

Without the animals circling around her, I finally have a chance to observe her outfit. She's wearing a simple tunic dress with cowboy boots. She's gorgeous. Juniper could wear a burlap sack and she'd be more beautiful than any Hollywood actress.

She squirms under my scrutiny. "I can change."

I step forward and grasp her hand. "Don't you dare. You look utterly gorgeous."

I kiss her knuckles and she shivers in response. I duck my head to hide my smug smile. I know she's affected by me – our chemistry has never been a problem – but the confirmation is welcome.

"Your chariot awaits." I motion to my golf cart.

"We can bike. We'll be just as fast and the only energy we'll use is our own leg power."

I ignore her and begin escorting her toward the driveway. But when I remember one of the reasons she doesn't trust me is because she thinks I don't share enough of myself with her, I realize I have to tell her the truth. No matter how embarrassing it is.

"I don't know how to ride a bike," I admit as I help her into the cart.

"I didn't realize. I'm sorry," she apologizes instead of making fun of me. And then she does the most wonderful thing of all, she lifts up and kisses my cheek.

I stand frozen for a moment enjoying the feel of her lips on my skin again. Her stomach grumbles, and I become unstuck. She giggles, completely unabashed by the sound of her stomach rumbling. She doesn't make any attempt to hide her true self from me. How refreshing.

I rush around the golf cart and jump in. The brewery is a few blocks away and we're there in no time. I frown when I notice the line outside the door.

"I didn't think to make a reservation."

"There's no need."

I allow her to drag me to the front of the line where she cuts in front of someone at the hostess station.

"Hey, Moon," she greets the woman. "Do you have a table for us?"

The hostess smiles at her before glancing over at me. Her eyes widen, but she doesn't otherwise comment on who I am. Again. Refreshing.

"You bet." She grabs two menus and marches off.

We follow her up the stairs to a corner booth. She slaps the menus on the table. "I'll be back to take your order in a while. It's a mad house today."

"What's going on?" Juniper asks before the hostess can leave.

"Love Hill didn't show up for her shift and now I'm stuck doing her work as well as mine."

Juniper stands. "Do you need my help?"

Moon waves for her to sit. "Don't be silly. I got this." She waggles her eyebrows. "Besides, you have a date."

As soon as she leaves, Juniper buries her face in her hands and groans.

"What's wrong?"

"Moon is Ashlyn's best friend. She's also competing to become the number one gossip of Winter Falls. News of our date is going to be around town before we're served our first beer."

I feel my forehead furrow as I study her. "Are you embarrassed of me?"

She bursts out laughing. "Are you serious? Me embarrassed of you?" She shakes her head. "You're hilarious."

"If you're not embarrassed, what's the problem?"

"You'll see," she sings but says no more as Moon returns to take our drink order.

Our beers haven't yet arrived when Sage darts into the room and runs to us before screeching to a halt in front of our table. She bends over at the waist and gulps for air.

"Told you. Before our first beer is served," Juniper teases.

"Is something wrong?" I ask Sage.

She throws her arms in the air. "Is something wrong, Rickie?" I cock an eyebrow at Juniper in the hope she can help me navigate this conversation, but she just shrugs. "Of course, something's wrong. I bet you wouldn't convince Juniper Berry to go on a date with you for another week. Another week! You're costing me money."

"Sage," Juniper growls. "You can't yell at Mav because you underestimated his ability to learn facts about the fennec fox."

"Fennec fox? What are you talking about?" She leans close to whisper, "Is this some new sex game?" She winks at me. "I guess I'll forgive you after all, Rickie." She saunters off without another word.

Moon arrives and sets two beers on our table. "Sorry. I couldn't catch her in time."

Juniper waves away the apology. "It's fine. *Rickie* is having a baptism by fire. It'll be good for him."

"You're mean." Moon giggles before asking what we want to eat. We order and she departs still giggling.

"Why is she laughing? What's funny?"

"You don't—"

Her words are cut off when Petal plops her purse down on our table. "I cannot believe you, Juniper Berry West. You're exploring new sex games and you didn't tell me! Where's the love? I had the candles picked out for you already."

She opens her bags and sets two candles down on the table before snapping her bag closed. "On the house, sugar." She winks at me before waving to someone across the room and walking off.

I pick up the first candle. Juniper bats it out of my grasp. "Don't encourage them."

"What'd I do? It's just a candle. What's the big deal?"

"It's not a candle."

I peer closer at it. "It sure looks like a candle."

Juniper squirms in her seat and my attention rivets on her. Why is she squirming and what can I do to make her squirm some more?

"It's a sex candle." I remain silent as I'm having too much fun watching her blush and squirm. Juniper rushes to fill the silence. "You use it for candle play. You know – drip hot wax on your body."

I don't get a chance to tell her I know exactly how hot wax play works – I starred in a movie with a heavy BDSM theme after all – when Moon arrives at our table.

"You're safe. I've kicked all the gossip gals out."

"How the hell did you manage it?" Juniper asks.

Moon smirks. "I told them I spotted Rowan and Ashlyn making out in the alley."

"You are mean. And Ashlyn's going to kick your butt."

"Then, she shouldn't have kept the gossip about you and Rickie here to herself."

I sit back and enjoy their banter. I missed this when I was sneaking around town thinking no one knew who I was; thinking spending time with Juniper alone was all we needed. I was wrong. We need this, too. To be part of her community.

And now I've had a glimpse of how good it feels to be included, there's no way I'm not going to do everything in my power to win Juniper back. She glances across the table at me and smiles. All of her smiles will be mine in the future.

Chapter 14

A cat is a puzzle for which there is no solution.

I OPEN THE DOOR to find all four of my sisters standing on the stoop. "What are you doing here? I was just on my way to *Fall Into A Good Book* for book club."

Lies. Lies. Lies. I was just on my way to thinking up an emergency to avoid book club. My sisters never skip book club since the meetings are always held at Aspen's bookstore, but there's no way I'm sitting in a room with my sisters and the gossip gals after going on a date with Mav.

Especially since said date ended with the lamest goodnight kiss ever despite how much I could feel Mav wanted me. Men! Way too complicated for their own good.

Gah! What am I thinking? I don't want a steamy goodnight kiss from Mav. It was one date because I lost a bet. We aren't back together. *But you want to be.* I mentally slap my head to force out any thoughts of Mav and me as a couple. I am not living in la la land.

"She's pretending we don't know she was planning on ducking out of book club," Aspen announces before marching inside. Ashlyn, Lilac, and Ellery follow her in.

"Come on in, why don't you?"

"Thank you," Lilac says in all seriousness.

"I was being sarcastic," I tell her.

She huffs. "I'm aware."

I'm not certain she's being truthful – my sister is part robot after all – but I let it slide. I've got bigger issues at the moment. Such as why are my sisters invading my house? Time for some evasion tactics.

"Where's Willow?" I ask Ellery.

"Where's Willow?" she mimics. "Does no one care about me anymore? Am I merely a vessel for a tiny human being whose sole capabilities are sleeping, screaming, and dirtying diapers in the most disgusting ways you can imagine?"

"There's no beer in your fridge," Aspen hollers from the kitchen where she's searching my refrigerator.

A cork pops. "There's wine." Ashlyn holds up a bottle of red.

"I guess we're drinking wine," I mumble as I gather wine glasses.

"None for me." Ellery motions toward her breasts. "These things are shooting milk for the baby."

I fill a glass with water and hand it to her. "Or do you want a soda?"

She sighs. "I would love a soda, but Cole would lose his ever-loving mind if he found out I drank one. Here's a tip. Never let the father of your baby read a baby book. Never. He's an architect, not a doctor, but he thinks he's an expert on babies now."

"I think it's attentive of Cole," Lilac says. "He's interested in you and the baby. You should be happy he's not ignoring you."

Her words make my Spidey-senses tingle. "Is someone ignoring you, Lilac?"

She frowns. "No. But I have been too busy to meet up with any of the men with whom I have arrangements lately."

Lilac's idea of romance is having romantic liaisons with men during her lunch break. There's no dating, no sharing of a meal together. I don't think she even talks to them. It's no-strings sex and nothing more.

"Too busy? Is your work busier than normal? Is the biomass project not going well?"

My brainiac sister is in charge of setting up a biomass energy source outside of town. The idea is to provide more clean energy to Winter Falls.

"The project is on schedule."

"Then, why are you too busy to meet up with your paramours?"

She purses her lips. "They are not paramours. No one is married or in a serious relationship."

I roll my eyes. "Whatever. Explain why you're too busy to meet with your sexual partners." Sexual partners. What a boring phrase. I hope there's more passion in the execution than in the description.

"My boss has given me more responsibility. I don't have time to have a lunch break when I'm meeting with him to discuss the project every day."

"Can you describe this boss of yours? Is he a broody but sexy man? Is he a billionaire? Does he stare at you with smoldering eyes like he wants to swallow you whole?"

Everyone turns to stare at Ashlyn. She throws her arms in the air. "Sorry. I'm in the middle of narrating a series of grumpy boss romances."

After studying drama in college, my baby sister decided she didn't want to be an actress. She wanted to narrate audiobooks instead. She specializes in erotic romances. And Rowan, being the devout husband he is, encouraged her career by building her a recording studio. He should know better than to encourage her.

Ellery settles onto my sofa and props her feet on the coffee table. "I thought we came here to discuss Juniper's date with Mav."

I know. Why do you think I'm trying to make Lilac's work troubles into a topic of discussion? I have no desire to have a discussion about my date with Mav with anyone, let alone my nosy sisters.

Ashlyn plops down on the sofa next to Ellery. "Let the interrogation begin."

And now you know why I don't want to discuss my date with them. "Interrogation? There's no need to interrogate me. You already know about the date."

She wiggles her eyebrows. "We know what happened at *Naked Falls Brewing*."

"Your friend, Moon, has the biggest mouth in all of Colorado."

She ignores me to continue her questioning, "What we don't know is what happened after he brought you home. Did you jump his bones? Did he jump yours? Did boots go knocking and headboards banging?"

"You enjoy sex rough, don't you?"

She wags her finger at me. "Nuh-uh. No deflecting on me. It's your turn. I've had mine." She waves her hand with her diamond wedding ring at me. "My turn was extremely successful."

"This is not my turn, and my sisters are not the matchmakers of Winter Falls."

Aspen snorts. "Of course, we're not. The gossip gals are. But we are your sisters, and we deserve to know what happened with Maverick."

I cock an eyebrow. "You *deserve* to know? The same way you told us why you hightailed it out of Winter Falls and left Lyric brokenhearted all those years ago."

"When are you going to let the past go?" she asks the room.

"I say never." Ellery's hand shoots into the air. "Who's with me?"

Ashlyn and I raise our hands. When Lilac doesn't, I raise an eyebrow at her. "Do I have to raise my hand? I am not in kindergarten."

"We're not here to talk about me," Aspen insists. "We're here to talk about what an idiot Juniper is being."

I rear back. "An idiot? I'm the idiot? You seriously thought—"

"Nope! We're not talking about my past. We're talking about you and Maverick now."

"There is no me and Maverick. We've been over for months now."

Ashlyn bats her eyelashes. "It didn't appear as if you were over at the brewery last night."

"I have it on good authority you weren't there."

She huffs. "I will get Moon back for tattling on me and Rowan if it's the last thing I do."

"Do you remember when I was being an idiot about Cole?" Ellery asks.

I nod because how could I forget? Ellery was a complete idiot. It was more than a little amusing to observe.

"What did you say to me at the time?"

I shrug. "I don't think I said anything. I'm pretty confident it was Aspen with her big mouth who did all the talking."

"Nevertheless. You pointed out what a bitch I was being to Cole."

I rear back. "Are you saying I'm a bitch?"

"She might not be, but I will," Ashlyn mutters, and I elbow her causing her wine to spill down her shirt.

"Hey! Watch it. This is the only clean shirt I have left."

"Not anymore it isn't."

"Children!" Ellery shouts.

"Whoa! Mama Ellery is in the house," Ashlyn grumbles.

Ellery glares at her for a moment before her gaze returns to me. "I'm not saying you're being a bitch. Not exactly, at least. But you aren't being very nice to Maverick."

"Did you forget about him kissing another woman in front of the entire world while he was with me?"

"I did some research on this," Lilac says.

My nose wrinkles, "Research on what? Kissing? Cheating?"

"On publicity stunts in Hollywood. It isn't unusual for stars to pretend to be in amorous relationships to boost the sales of a movie."

I rub a hand over my chest. "But why didn't he tell me it was a stunt?"

"Maybe he would have if you had picked up one of the gazillion times he phoned you," Ashlyn suggests.

Dang it. Is she right?

"What's to say he won't do it again?"

"Honestly?" Ashlyn asks, and I motion for her to continue. "I think it will happen again." I gasp. "Hold on before you get your panties in a bunch." I snap my teeth at her. "But you two can discuss it before it happens again, can't you? You don't go all jealous girlfriend on him when he kisses another woman in a movie, do you?"

"Of course, not. He's acting in a movie. I'm not an idiot."

"Think of this as the same thing. It's an act. Plain and simple." Ashlyn stands and downs the rest of her wine. "My work here is done."

Ellery clasps my hand. "Ashlyn may be crazy, but she's not wrong." When Ashlyn does a victory dance, she adds, "This time."

Everyone starts to leave.

"By the way," Aspen stops at the door. "When you see Maverick, can you tell him Lyric wasn't messing around?"

My brow wrinkles. "What are you talking about now?"

"Lyric caught Maverick driving his fancy schmancy car in town and pulled him over. Apparently, Maverick thought it was a joke," she explains.

"There's really no need to drive in Winter Falls," Lilac says. "He can use a golf cart. Or, better yet, he can bike."

"I'll tell him," I promise before shutting the door on my sisters and slumping against it.

I knew they'd invade after word of my date with Mav got around. I expected them to push me for details of our relationship, but what they did was worse. Way worse. They made me reconsider everything.

Am I being a bitch? Do I need to let the kissing incident go? And, if I do, how do I learn to trust Mav again and not get my heart broken once more.

Chapter 15

People who say money can't buy happiness have never paid a pet adoption fee.

I PARK THE BIKES on Mav's lawn and stare up at his house. Once upon a time, I thought the Colonial style house would become my home. The oversized fenced-in yard is perfect for my dogs, while the fancy kitchen with every appliance known to man would be perfect for me. Not to mention how I would die to relax in the clawfoot bathtub after a day of working at the Wildlife Refuge.

Snort. I was such an idiot. In what world would movie star Maverick Langston want me for his happily ever after? Not this one.

Shake it off, Juniper. This is not the moment to worry about what ifs. Not when I'm here on a mission I've dubbed 'stop being a bitch'.

I spent the night thinking and thinking and thinking some more about what my sisters said and came to the conclusion I definitely didn't want to come to. I'm being too hard on Mav. Was he wrong to kiss another woman? Yes. No doubt about it. But it wasn't real. Could he have warned me in advance?

Damn straight he could have. Am I holding on to my grudge because my feelings for Mav scare the living daylights out of me? Definitely.

Enough with being scared out of my mind. If I can face off with a pissed off cougar, I can definitely handle this. I march up the porch steps and knock on the door.

Mav's smile lights up his face when he answers. "June Bug."

Great. As if I weren't already feeling like an asshole, he has to grace me with his genuine smile. Ugh.

"I'm here to teach you how to ride a bike," I blurt out before I can tell him I want to have his babies. What am I thinking? I have lost my dang mind. It's the smile I tell you. It makes me think all kinds of crazy thoughts.

"What? Ride a bike?"

I indicate the bikes. "Not the vroom-vroom, I'm James Dean and cool in a t-shirt and jeans, bike. A bicycle with two wheels you have to pedal."

His lips twitch. "Vroom-vroom?"

"Shaddup. I've never taught someone to ride a bike before. I spent half the night watching YouTube videos. I'm tired and not thinking clearly." I pat my pants to check they don't light on fire after my ginormous lie.

"You didn't need to do that. I don't need to know how to ride a bike. I have the golf cart."

I cross my arms over my chest and watch as his gaze dips to my cleavage. I quickly drop my arms before my nipples pebble to show off how much I enjoy him gazing at my body like he can't wait to devour me. *Head out of the gutter, Juniper!*

"I heard from a very reliable source you've been driving your car in town."

He cocks an eyebrow and his eyes sparkle. Dang. Why does he have to be this handsome? "A very reliable source?"

"If you're planning to stay in town, you best learn now Winter Falls is a bed of gossip." I pause. "Assuming you are planning to stay."

"My plans haven't changed, June Bug. I'm here to stay."

My belly warms at his declaration. Maverick Langston around town 365 days a year? I could learn to love him being here permanently. *Learn to love? Really, Juniper? You need to stop lying to yourself.*

"In which case, you should learn to ride a bike."

"Do I have to?" he whines.

I scrunch my nose as I study his stiff posture. "Are you afraid?"

He growls. "No."

"Alrighty then. Let's do this." I march to the bikes and gesture toward the one I borrowed for him. He retreats with his hands up. "I can't learn on this bike. It's a girl's bike."

"Beep! Wrong. All bikes are unisex. The only difference is size and fit." When he doesn't appear any closer to wanting to come near, I decide to try a different tactic. "I never thought I'd witness the day Maverick Langston was a chicken." I tap my cheek. "Oh wait. There was the time he ran away from a giant, adorable rodent."

He growls. "Those capybaras have it out for me."

I giggle. "Sure, they do."

"Fine. What do I do?"

I grin, but I don't jump for joy in victory. I'll pencil 'jumping for joy' in my diary for later.

"Straddle the bike."

He wiggles his eyebrows. "I can think of something else I'd rather be straddling."

"Oh, my dork. It's too early for sleazy sexual innuendos."

He chuckles as he straddles the bike. "What now?"

"Now, you're going to walk with the bike."

"Walk? Shouldn't I use the pedals?" He places a foot on the pedal and pushes down causing the bike to lurch forward. He loses his balance and ends up falling to his side.

I rush to him. "Are you okay?" I lift the bike off of him.

"If I say no, can we stop?"

"I never figured you for a quitter."

He climbs to his feet and brushes his jeans off. "I am not a quitter."

"Good." I nod in approval. "Let's try this again."

"I don't understand why I have to walk with the bike. I'm not a two-year-old," he grouses as he walks down the sidewalk with the bike between his legs.

"You're getting the feel of the bike. Once you have the feel of the bike, you can speed up and scoot with the bike."

"Finally." He lifts his foot to place it on the pedal.

"Nuh-uh. No using the pedals yet. You're going to scoot faster and faster until you have to lift your legs."

"I feel like an idiot," he says but does as he's told.

"Why didn't you learn to bike as a kid?" I ask when he stops for a break.

"My parents wouldn't let me."

I rear back. "Wouldn't let you? What type of parents don't let their child learn to ride a bike?"

"The type with a child actor who might lose a commercial gig if he has a scraped knee."

"So what? You lose one commercial. What's the big deal?"

"The big deal was I was their meal ticket."

He pushes off to start scooting with the bike again, but I grab the handlebars to stop him.

"You supported your parents with your acting when you were a child? Didn't they have jobs?"

"My mother was a stay-at-home mom. She took me to all my auditions. When I began to earn decent money, Dad quit his job at the hardware store."

He scowls at the memory, and I reach forward to squeeze his hand without thinking about it. "Did you even want to be an actor?"

"Too late now." He pushes off with his feet and glides down the sidewalk before I have a chance to respond. Message received. The topic of discussion is now closed. Got it.

"Lift your feet," I shout after him. "And balance the bike."

I clap when he does as I say and manages not to crash. "You're a natural," I tell him when he reaches me. He smirks, and I roll my eyes. "Don't get cocky now. You haven't technically ridden a bike yet."

I wait until the humor in his eyes is replaced with seriousness before I explain, "Put your right foot on the pedal and slowly push down. Once the bike is moving, put your left foot on the pedal while focusing forward and balancing the bike."

"Got it," he claims before putting both feet on the pedals at once and pitching to the side. I grab the bike frame in an attempt to stop his fall and end up crushed under the bike and him.

"Shit. Shit. Juniper. Are you okay?" Mav scrambles to his feet before picking the bike off of me and reaching out a hand to help me up.

"I'm fine. You didn't hit me full speed."

"And here I thought you would be the one to kiss my boo-boos today."

Why does the idea of kissing his boo-boos make me feel all hot and bothered? My body is such a slut for the movie star.

"It's all good," I say as I brush my hands off. "I don't have any boo-boos for you to kiss."

"Darn." He curls his bottom lip in a pout.

"Let's try this again," I bark before I decide biting his bottom lip is a great idea. "You will learn how to ride a bike today."

"Yes, Sergeant West."

"How come I'm a sergeant? I could be an officer."

He ignores me and climbs on the bike again. "Listen to my directions this time," I order before repeating the instructions.

He wobbles as he begins to pedal. I hold onto the seat and follow him. "You need to pick up speed. It's hard to balance when you're biking this slow."

He glances back at me. "No! Don't look at me. Focus forward."

I push on the bike seat to increase his momentum and he picks up speed. He pedals in earnest now, and I chase after him.

"You're doing it! You're riding a bike!"

He glances over his shoulder at me. "I am!"

His hands follow the movement of his head and the bike veers to the left before hitting a patch of grass causing the bike to careen to a stop. He doesn't get the chance to steady himself before he's flying over the handlebars. I rush forward and try to catch him, but we end up in a heap of arms and legs on the ground.

He rolls us until he's looming over me. "Finally. I have you precisely where I want you."

I can't catch my breath as I stare up at him. "And where's that?"

"In my arms," he whispers before his head descends and his lips find mine.

At the first touch, I sigh and open up for him. It's been entirely too long since I've felt his lips on mine. His tongue darts in and mine reaches out to duel with his. His hands thread through my hair to hold my head the exact way he wants, and he takes over. He doesn't build the kiss up. Not my Mav. He plunders from the start.

He continues to plunder until we're both gasping for breath and my fingers are embedded in his t-shirt holding him close to me.

He smiles down at me. "There she is. I've missed you, June Bug."

June Bug? Missed me? Holy balls of puppy chow!

What am I doing? I didn't come here to re-ignite our love affair. I planned to teach him how to ride a bike and maybe rekindle our friendship – not stick my tongue down his throat. I release his t-shirt and shove at his shoulders until he rolls away. As soon as I can, I spring to my feet and sprint to my bike.

I jump on and pedal away before I end up making a bigger mistake – falling in love with Mav again. He broke my heart once. What's to say he won't do it again?

Chapter 16

If it sounds like a duck, has a bill like a duck, webbed feet like a duck, and swims like a duck, you should still make sure it's not a platypus.

MAVERICK

"Welcome!" Ashlyn greets me as I enter the town hall.

I stare at her in confusion. "What are you doing here? I'm supposed to be meeting the mayor."

She beams at me. "I am the mayor."

"You're the mayor?" I glance around the empty town hall. "Am I being punked?"

"Why? Because you can't believe I could be the mayor?" She crosses her arms over her chest and huffs. "I'll have you know I'm a legitimate business owner. You may have heard of my place – Bertie's Recording Studio. I can fulfill all of your recording wishes and dreams."

Is she serious? Bertie's Recording Studio is gaining quite the reputation amongst indie recording artists, but the location is a closely guarded industry secret. I had no idea the studio is in Winter Falls.

"You own Bertie's Recording Studio?"

She bows. "I do."

"And you're the mayor?"

Now, she curtseys. "At your service."

"I guess you're the person I need to speak to about donating to the community center project."

She bounces on her toes. "Yeah! I knew you were a good guy. I can't wait to tell Juniper."

"You can't tell Juniper."

She wrinkles her nose. "Why not?"

"I want my donation to be confidential."

Her lips purse. "I didn't sign up for confidential when I volunteered as tribute. Which reminds me, I need to buy a Hunger Games costume."

I scratch my beard. What in the world is she talking about? And here I thought Juniper was exaggerating when she told me her baby sister is crazy. "Tribute?"

The doors open behind me and a man wheels in several crates of beer.

"No time to explain. The Winter Fall's monthly business meeting is about to begin."

"I'll leave you to it."

She grabs my sleeve before I can escape. "Oh no, you don't. You're a business owner in town. You should attend."

"She's right, Rickie," Sage agrees as she enters. "Business owners should attend the monthly meetings when they're in town."

"Plus, Juniper will be here. Showing her you're interested in the town is a good way to win her back." Feather winks.

"Speaking of which, how long do you think it will be before you win her back?" Petal asks.

Cayenne slaps her. "You can't ask him how much time he needs. It's cheating."

I'm nearly afraid to ask. "Cheating? What would she be cheating at?"

The gossip gals giggle before sitting in the back of the room. What they don't do is answer my question.

"What are they talking about?" I ask Ashlyn.

She bats her eyelashes. "What do you mean?"

"Has anyone ever told you you're a horrible liar?"

She plants her fists on her hips and grunts. "I'll have you know I am an excellent liar. I graduated at the top of my class in drama school. Just because we're not all big Hollywood stars doesn't mean we're talentless hacks. And here I've been defending you to my sister, Aspen."

I obviously touched a nerve. "Sorry. I didn't mean to—"

She bursts out laughing. "Got you."

Rowan, Lyric, and Cole enter the room. Rowan makes a beeline for Ashlyn. "Dream girl," he mutters. "Are you causing trouble?"

Ashlyn stops laughing to glare up at her husband. "I am not causing trouble. I'm the mayor, remember?"

"You do know being the mayor isn't a get out of jail free card?" Aspen asks her baby sister.

Aspen's here? Maybe Juniper is as well. I scan the room for her.

"Juniper's not here yet. Something about Bark Twain being sick," Ellery answers my unasked question. "And before anyone asks, Willow is with Mom and Dad."

"But I want my cuddles," Ashlyn pouts.

"Have your own baby if you want baby cuddles."

"I'm working on it," Ashlyn grumbles.

"I believe it's time to begin the meeting," Lilac says as she taps her watch.

"Who's the mayor here? Me or you?" Ashlyn asks before she kisses Rowan and bounces to the front of the room.

I settle on a chair in the second row next to Rowan.

"At least with Ashlyn trying to get pregnant, we don't have to play the silly drinking game," Lilac says as she sits down in the row in front of me.

"We don't?" Juniper plunks a bucket of beer down at the end of the row.

"Why do my sisters insist on being childish?" Lilac grumbles.

"I'm not childish. I'm thirsty." Aspen motions to the bucket. "Give me a beer, will you?"

Juniper hands Aspen and Lilac a beer. "Today's word is 'never'."

"Never say never," Aspen sings before sipping on her beer.

Lilac frowns but takes a sip on her beer as well.

"June Bug," I call to gain Juniper's attention.

Bang! Bang! Bang! Ashlyn pounds a gavel on the front table before Juniper can respond to me. "Hear ye. Hear ye. The May meeting of the Winter Falls business community shall now begin."

"Does she think we're living in the nineteenth century?" Juniper whispers.

"The expression 'hear ye, hear ye' dates back to the British Parliament in the 1600s," Lilac explains.

"I never knew." Juniper smirks. "Drink up."

Bang! "First order of business is the community center."

Cole and Lilac stand before joining Ashlyn at the front of the room.

"Cole as architect and project manager of the community center will give us a brief update on the project before Lilac reports on the finances."

"Cole! Cole! Cole!" The gossip gals are on their feet shouting and whistling.

Ellery moans. "I thought they'd calm down after we got back together."

"What does she mean?" I ask Rowan.

"The gossip gals consider themselves the matchmakers of Winter Falls and take credit for getting Cole and Ellery together."

Tell me something I don't know.

"Except I was pregnant with Cole's baby, and they didn't know it." Ellery appears mighty proud of herself for pulling one over on the busybodies.

"Ahem." Cole clears his throat loudly. He shakes his head at Ellery before continuing, "As you know, we broke ground on the site last week, which means we're on schedule. The foundation will be poured next week."

"Thus far, we've raised approximately sixty percent of the funds necessary to build the community center," Lilac adds. "It's enough to begin construction, but we need to think about ways we can raise funds to ensure the construction doesn't halt."

"I have an idea," Ashlyn says, and her gaze falls on me. I squirm in my seat.

"I already donated," Rowan shouts out from next to me. "I'm happy to donate more, but my accountant says I have to wait until the next fiscal year before making any further donations."

Ashlyn continues to stare in my direction. I don't need to scan the room to know the rest of the town is now looking in my direction. Knowing when I'm under scrutiny is a skill I acquired years ago when I moved to Hollywood – a place where your every move is tracked by the paparazzi.

I keep my mouth shut until Juniper turns around. "What is Ashlyn trying to say?"

"I think she's saying she doesn't know how to keep a secret."

"I never agreed to keep our discussion confidential," Ashlyn hollers.

"Oh, Rickie, I'm so proud of you," Sage yells from the back of the room, and I realize I've lost the battle.

I stand. "I'll donate the remaining amount."

Everyone in the room applauds but the only person's opinion I care about is sitting right in front of me. She stares at me as she sets her beer down on the floor. She continues to hold my gaze as she slowly gets to her feet before climbing onto her chair and launching herself at me.

I catch her and she wraps herself around me like a monkey. "Thank you, Mav." She plants kisses along my face. "Thank you." Kiss. "Thank you." Kiss.

As much as I'm enjoying her attention, she doesn't need to thank me. "You don't need to thank me."

She leans back. "Of course, I do. The center is important to the community."

"Huh. I guess the mystery of why it's called a community center is now solved," I tease.

She slaps my shoulder. "Don't tease me."

"As I recall, you enjoy it when I tease you," I murmur, and her body jolts in my arms.

Her cheeks darken as she bites her lip. I can feel her chest rise and fall as she fights for breath, and I decide to push my luck.

"You know how you can thank me? Let me take you out tomorrow."

"I have to work at the refuge tomorrow."

"I already asked Harmony to fill in," I say and wait for her to yell at me for being presumptuous.

"Okay," she breathes out.

"Okay?"

She nods and I lower my head intent on tasting her. Before her lips can meet mine, Rowan slaps me on the back, and I nearly drop Juniper.

I growl at him, and he nods toward the gossip gals who are not trying to hide how they're watching us. Shit. He's right. This isn't the place to reacquaint myself with the taste of Juniper's lips.

I set her on the ground. "Until tomorrow, June Bug."

Chapter 17

What happened to the geese that fell down the stairs? They got goose bumps.

AT THE KNOCK ON my door, I race toward it but before I reach it, I remember to not appear too eager. I don't want Mav thinking he can get anything he wants from me with a snap of his fingers. I mean, he can. But there's no need for me to advertise it.

As much as I pretend we're just friends, my body wants to jump from the 'just friends' pasture straight into the 'sexy times' pasture. According to it, the grass is greener on the other side of the fence *and* it's way more fun, too.

I inhale a deep breath and calm myself before opening the door. Mav stands on my porch appearing absolutely delectable in a t-shirt and shorts. The summer outfit showcases his lean muscles. He isn't one of those action heroes who look like they eat steroids for breakfast. He's fit and lean in a natural way.

"Hey, June Bug," he greets before leaning forward to kiss my cheek. "I thought we'd go for a bike ride and have a nice—"

"A p-i-c-n-i-c?" I cut him off before he can say the word.

"Yes, a picnic."

I slap a hand over his mouth, but it's too late – the p-word is already out.

Bark Twain and Indiana Bones come barreling into the living room and don't stop until they reach me. Their tails wag and they stare up at me with their puppy dog eyes.

"No!" I command causing the barking to end and the howling to begin. I kneel down and pet my babies. "I'm sorry, my sweet things, but you aren't coming with me today."

Meowise huffs from the neck of the hallway before twirling around and prancing away. She doesn't need to speak for me to understand how pissed she is at me. I hope I locked away my shoes. Otherwise, she won't hesitate to show me her disdain for being left home alone with the dogs. There aren't enough shoes in the world for me to handle her disdain each time she's left home with them.

"I'm sorry. I didn't realize pi—" He cuts himself off. "The p-word was a sensitive one."

"It's fine. They're just being big babies."

I back up until I'm on the porch before I shut the door. I nearly shut it in Bark Twain's snout, but he pulls back at the last second the same way he does every time.

"Are you sure you're up to a long bike ride? You've been riding a bike for a grand total of a week."

He mumbles an answer.

"What did you say?"

He sighs. "I said I've been practicing every day."

I ignore his embarrassment. Why is he embarrassed about practicing? Practicing makes perfect.

"Great. There's a nice bike trail around town. It passes the falls. Have you been to the falls yet?"

In the past when Mav visited Winter Falls, he mostly kept to his house or the Wildlife Refuge as he didn't want anyone knowing he was in town. He said he was 'keeping a low profile'. Silly man. As if the entire town didn't know he owned the refuge anyway. You can't keep anything secret in this town. No matter how sneaky you think you're being.

"Lead the way," he says as he climbs on his bike.

I notice the bike isn't one of the loaners anyone can borrow from around town. The loaners are all simple bikes with no gears and are painted bright yellow. This bike is a matte black. "Did you buy a bike?"

"It's sexy, isn't it?"

I should have known. Mav doesn't do anything by half measures. Of course, he went from not knowing how to ride a bike to buying a sexy ass bike in a week. The man has exactly one speed – as fast as possible – except when we were in bed. Then, he has lots of different speeds.

"Let's go," I croak out and mount my bike before I decide testing Mav on all his speeds is the best idea ever.

I lead him toward the recreational bike path. The path is mostly flat and isn't too long. Perfect for someone who learned to bike last week.

As we pedal along, I fill Mav in on some of the plant and animal life in the area. "Did you know trees are one of the oldest species on this planet? They're estimated to be over 400 million years old. The experts believe trees first developed from fungi that could grow up to twenty-six feet wide."

"I did not know." Mav chuckles. "I also didn't know what a geek you are."

I roll my eyes. "Really? You had no clue I'm a plant and animal geek?"

"Animal geek I knew. Anyone who can love a capybara must be an animal nut."

"Capybaras are adorable and affectionate."

"They're also out to get me."

"You need to get over what happened. Every animal handler has been bit at least once in their lifetime. If you want to spend more time at the refuge, you can't be scared of the animals."

He doesn't respond and I backpedal. Not literally – I have no intention of wiping out in front of him – but figuratively. "Assuming you want to stay in Winter Falls and be more involved in the refuge."

His breaks squeak as he brings his bike to a halt. "June Bug," he calls out and I stop my bike as well.

He reaches over and grasps my hand. "What do I have to do to convince you I'm here to stay?"

I shrug because I don't know. I feel like a teenager with a crush on the football quarterback while I'm the science nerd – insecure and unsure of myself.

"I'm not going to lie and tell you I'm giving up my career. I'm not. But I do plan to spend as much time in Winter Falls as possible. It's my home base now."

"Your home base? Isn't Hollywood your base?"

"Nope. I plan to sell my house in Hollywood. I don't need to hobnob with other celebrities and producers anymore. I've worked hard on my career and proved to them I can bring in the fans."

My jaw drops. "You're seriously selling your house?"

He doesn't hesitate to answer, "I am."

I swallow. "Okay. I will try harder to believe you're in Winter Falls to stay."

He leans across the bikes and kisses my cheek. "Thank you."

A bike bell rings from behind us, and I startle. A public bike path is not the place to have a serious discussion. "Come on. I know the perfect place to have our picnic."

We ride to the falls after which Winter Falls is named. I know the second Mav notices it because I hear him gasp. The falls are pretty amazing. I stop my bike to watch him. His mouth is gaping open as he stares at the waterfall. He pulls out his phone and takes a few pictures.

When he finishes, I lead him to the grassy clearing at the top of the falls. "This is one of my favorite places in the world," I tell him as I spread a blanket over the grass for our picnic.

He wraps an arm around my waist and pulls me close until my back is plastered to his front. My body warms in delight at being in his arms again as he kisses my neck causing goose-bumps to break out across my skin.

"Thank you for sharing your favorite place with me," he whispers against my ear, and I tilt my head to the side to give him access to the sensitive skin below my ear. His tongue swirls a circle against my skin before he places a kiss there.

"A-a-re you hungry?" I manage to ask.

"Starving," he growls. I don't think he's talking about food.

"We should …" My words trail off when he spins me around.

He palms my neck and leans down to whisper into my ear, "We should what?"

I bite my lip and contemplate giving in and telling him exactly what I want, but a chirp sounds before I can give into my desires. I scan the area.

Mav releases me. "What's wrong?"

"I hear chirping. I think an animal is in distress."

I drop to my knees and crawl to the brush. The chirping intensifies. I must be getting closer. I spot a striped skunk about three feet away.

"Hey, little guy. What's wrong? Are you hurt?"

"Maybe it's mating season and he's trying to attract a female."

"Mating season ends in mid-March," I tell him as I crawl closer.

"Maybe you should keep your distance."

"I'm not abandoning an injured animal in the wild when I can help him."

"I should have known better," he mutters.

"Stay back," I warn when I hear him trampling through the bush.

"I'm not going to let you face an animal without me by your side."

"Keep it down. You're scaring him."

"Me? I'm scaring him? He's the one with the beady eyes who's going to spray us any minute."

"He won't unless he feels threatened. Besides, he needs to turn around to spray us."

I drop to my stomach and begin to crawl on my belly toward the skunk. "Hey, little guy. I'm here to help you. Are you stuck?"

"Here," Mav says, "I have my Swiss Army knife."

"Stay back," I warn him again when he stomps my way. He couldn't make any more noise if he tried to.

The skunk chirps loudly before turning around, lifting his tale, and spurting his poison at me. I close my eyes as I scramble backwards out of the shrubs as fast as I can.

"Love a duck," I swear as I gasp for unpolluted air.

"What do I do? Do I need to take you to the hospital?"

"I don't need a hospital. I need a shower."

"And you need tomato juice."

"Tomato juice is a myth," I say as I mount my bike. "I'm going home." At least I managed to save my eyes from the spray. Otherwise, I'd be too blind to walk, let alone bike home.

"What are you doing?" I ask when Mav pedals next to me as I hurry home.

"I'm ensuring you get home safe."

I don't have time to argue with him. I continue to pedal until I reach my house. I don't bother putting my bike in the garage. I drop it on the ground and hurry inside. My dogs rush toward me, but when they get a whiff of me, they scatter. I can't blame them. I stink to high heaven.

I jump in the shower with my clothes on. They're as polluted as I am. As soon as the clothes are good and wet, I shed them. I hear the bathroom door squeak open and yell out, "Not now, my sweet things. Mama needs a shower."

"How can I help?"

I scream and wrap the shower curtain around my naked body. "What are you doing in here, Mav?"

"I'm helping."

"I don't need your help. I have a mixture to get rid of the stench." I wave my hand toward the bottle.

He chuckles. "How often have you been sprayed by skunks that you have a mixture prepared?"

More than I ever want to admit, so I don't. "Shaddup."

He climbs into the shower fully dressed. "I told you I don't need your help."

"I don't care. You're getting it. Now, turn around so I can rinse your hair with whatever witches' brew you've prepared."

I stay frozen where I am. If I move, I'll have to unwrap the shower curtain and expose my body to him. Sure, he's seen it before. But not while I'm dealing with a skunk attack, and he's fully dressed.

"I didn't take you for a chicken."

No one calls me a chicken. I drop the curtain and step under the water to wet my hair.

Dang it. When am I going to learn to not accept a challenge?

Chapter 18

Imagine how excited barn owls were when people invented barns.

MAVERICK

When Juniper drops the curtain and ducks her head under the water, I blow out a silent breath of relief. My June Bug is the most stubborn person in the world. She'd stand here for hours waiting for the water to turn cold if she wanted to.

"Tilt your head back, June Bug."

"There's a pair of gloves hanging on the towel rack. You should use them or my witches' brew as you named it will irritate your hands."

I glove up – but not in the way I'd prefer to when I have a naked Juniper West in the shower with me – and pour the solution over her hair. I ensure her hair is completely covered with the mixture before moving on to her body.

As thoroughly as I can, I scrub her body with the mixture while being careful not to overexpose her skin. I'm thankful for the gloves – not because I'm worried about irritating my skin – but because the layer of protection prevents me from feeling her silky smooth skin.

There's no way I can touch her naked body without my body responding and the last thing she needs now is a man with a hard-on in her shower while dealing with the result of a skunk attacking her.

"I would have been fine, you know," she murmurs while I'm on my knees scrubbing her feet and ankles.

"Fine how?" I ask and glance up at her.

Mistake. Big mistake. I may not be able to feel her while wearing these idiotic gloves, but I certainly can view the miles upon miles of naked skin. I drop my gaze before I begin drooling. I am not an untouched high school kid, but she sure makes me feel as if I am.

"If you hadn't trampled through the bush with your over-sized feet and big mouth, the skunk would have never sprayed me."

"Hmm…" I mumble since I know she's correct.

I acted like an idiot rushing in to protect my woman when she was perfectly fine without me. She always is, and it rankles. I don't want a simpering woman, but it would be nice to know Juniper needs me half as much as I do her.

"I think we're done," Juniper says once she's rinsed the mixture out of her hair and off of her skin.

Done? I thought we were starting over. "What?"

"You've scrubbed every single inch of my body. I can handle things from here."

Oh. She's talking about the shower. I have no plans to let her handle things, though.

I smirk up at her. "Does this mean I can ditch the gloves and put my hands on your skin?"

She shivers and her nipples tighten. I rip off the gloves and throw them on the shower floor before placing my hands on her ankles. I wait for her nod before drawing my hands up her legs as I stand.

I palm her cheeks. "Are you sure?"

"Am I sure about what?" Her eyes twinkle as she teases me.

"Are you sure you want me to worship your naked body?"

She shivers. "I don't know. What's in it for me?"

"Oh, I can think of a thing … or two." I wink.

"Two?" She cocks her eyebrow. "Is that a promise?"

"Damn straight it is," I growl.

"If we do this." I freeze at the insecurity clear to hear in her voice, "there will be no more kissing other women. If you need to kiss another woman for a promo stunt, I *will* know about it beforehand, and we *will* discuss it before your lips touch another person."

Fuck, I'm an idiot. What was I thinking agreeing to do a promotion stunt just because the producer wanted the film to hit number one in the cinemas the next weekend? As if the film wasn't already grossing millions.

Lesson learned. No more promo stunts. At least not any-where I have to pretend to be someone I'm not. Or act as if I'm in love with someone I'm not. There's only one woman I love in this world and I'm staring right at her.

"Agreed."

Her shoulders sag in relief at my agreement and I'm done waiting. I crash my lips onto hers and she immediately opens for me. Her taste of strawberries and wilderness hits me, and I moan. I could kiss her all day long. All night, too, for that matter, if she'd let me.

She rubs up against me like a cat in heat and I remember I'm still fully dressed. I lean back to remove my top and throw it on the floor of the bathtub. I barely manage to untangle my arms before Juniper palms my neck and forces my mouth down to meet hers again. Her eagerness sends a thrill of excitement through my body.

Our lips collide and our teeth clash. She nips my bottom lip and I growl down her mouth. Her taste isn't the only thing wild about her.

I pick her up and wait for her legs to circle my waist. As soon as she's wrapped around me, I press her against the wall. The water from the shower hits me in the face and I sputter.

She giggles as I reach down to switch off the water. "Shower sex isn't as sexy as the movies make it out to be."

"You don't think this is sexy?" I punch my hips allowing my hardness to hit her center.

She moans and arches her back as she grinds herself on my hardness. My fingers dig into her thighs, and I use my hold to drag her up and down my length.

"Holy cow, I forgot how good this feels."

"Been a while, June Bug?"

She doesn't stop her movements as she answers, "You know exactly how long it's been."

At her confirmation she hasn't been with anyone since me, relief hits me, and I have to lock my knees before I crumble to the bottom of the shower with her in my arms.

"It's the same for me."

She stills at my admission before dipping her chin to meet my gaze. "It is?"

"You didn't honestly think I've been pushing for you to give me a second chance while I had another woman on the side, did you?"

She shrugs. "I don't know. You kissed another woman."

I growl, and she raises a palm.

"I know. I know. It wasn't how it appeared, but I didn't know the truth until recently, did I?"

"I'm sorry, June Bug. I'm so damn sorry. I messed up."

She soothes her hands across my shoulders. "It's okay. We all mess up sometimes."

My body jolts with relief at her forgiveness. Finally. My eyes fall closed and I rest my forehead against hers. All the hard work to get her to forgive me was worth it for this moment.

"Thank you," I whisper against her skin.

"You can thank me by removing the rest of your clothes and beginning the worshipping my body portion of the day."

I smirk before stepping out of the tub. I carry her in my arms as I walk into to her bedroom. She huffs when her gaze catches on the bed.

"You didn't shut the door to my bedroom?"

Shutting the door was the last thing on my mind as I hurried to the shower to help her.

I shrug. "At least, they didn't interrupt us in the bathroom."

"Let me down." At her command, I tighten my hold. "Just until I deal with these rugrats."

I frown but release her to allow her to stand. She plants her hands on her hips causing her chest to jut forward and I promise myself to never forget to shut her bedroom door again. No more interruptions.

"Bark Twain, Indiana Bones, get!"

They lift their heads from where they've made themselves comfortable in the bed but don't make any move to leave.

"Now," she growls and gestures toward the door.

They both bark before jumping down from the bed and running out of the room.

She snaps her fingers. "You too, Meowise."

The cat doesn't bother to glance up from licking her paw.

"Fine." She stomps to the cat and reaches forward to pick her up. The cat swipes at her with a hiss before springing from the bed and stalking off.

She shuts the door behind the cat and turns to me. "Now, where were we?"

"What about Dale?" The chipmunk is perched on top of her dresser.

"He won't bother us."

"I—" My protest dies in my mouth as she struts toward me causing her breasts to jiggle. Let the stupid chipmunk watch while I pleasure my woman. I couldn't care less about the rodent right now.

Juniper stops in front of me. She bites her bottom lip as she glides a finger down my chest. "I think someone is wearing entirely too many clothes."

I capture her wrists before she can unbutton my shorts. "I can worship your body without being naked."

"We'll save the worshipping for the second round," she says, and snaps open my shorts. She shoves the wet material along with my boxers down my legs and I step out of them.

She looks up at my cock from beneath her eyelashes and licks her lips. I groan before bending down to grab her underneath her arms. "Not this time."

I throw her on the bed before climbing on top of her. "This first time is gonna be quick."

She spreads her legs and I fit my hips between them. My cock immediately finds her wet heat. She wraps her legs around my waist and her heels dig into my ass. It's all I can do to stop myself from slamming into her.

But I want to remember this moment. The moment I finally have my woman where she should have been all along. I take my time sinking into her. Her fingers dig into my shoulders while her back arches and her head falls back with a groan.

"I missed this," she pants when I'm fully seated. "I missed feeling filled by you."

"I missed you, too," I whisper before my mouth has better things to do such as licking and biting my way across her shoulder to her neck.

She wiggles underneath me. "Are you going to move?"

My teeth latch on to her collarbone. "I am moving."

She growls. "You know what I meant."

I ignore her and continue nibbling on her skin.

She squeezes me with her inner muscles, and I groan. "You're cheating."

"And you're a big, fat tease."

"I'm a tease?" I pull out and freeze with the tip of my cock inside her.

"You know you are."

I thrust into her. "Is this teasing?" I ask as I pull out of her before thrusting in again. I find my rhythm and I forget all about teasing her. Who has time for teasing when the feel of her wrapped around me is the best thing I've ever felt in my life?

"Mav, honey," Juniper repeats over and over until she loses the ability to speak altogether.

Her body seizes before her back bows as her nails dig into my skin and she shouts her release. At the feel of her muscles squeezing me, I nearly lose my mind. My rhythm fails and my movements become erratic as I fall off the cliff and my climax hits me.

"June, baby," I sigh as I stay planted and release inside her.

I collapse on top of her before rolling us until she's cuddled into my side.

"I love you," I whisper into her hair. When she doesn't respond, I brush the hair away from her face to discover she's fast asleep. Figures. I finally get the courage up to confess my feelings and she's dead to the world.

Chapter 19

There's only one animal that lies – humans.

I wake cocooned in a blanket of warmth. I haven't slept this good in ages. I snuggle into my pillow and blanket. The blanket moans and I freeze. Hell and damnation. I'm not wrapped in a blanket. I'm wrapped in Mav.

What have I done? What kind of idiot am I? The plan was to slowly work our way toward being friends again before – maybe – adding romance to the mix. The plan was not to jump into bed with him at the first opportunity.

Mav brushes my hair from my face. "Stop overthinking things," he whispers before kissing the spot behind my ear.

I suppress the shiver from his kiss. "I am not overthinking things."

"Uh-huh. You went from languid in my arms to frozen stiff for no reason at all."

I force myself to relax. "I was surprised you're still in bed with me is all. Usually, you depart post-haste the minute the exciting times are over."

He growls before rolling me until he's looming over me. "One time. One damn time. You need to stop bringing up the past if you want to go forward."

I blow out a breath of air. I hate it when he's right. Actually, I hate it when anyone dares to point out I've made a mistake. Having four sisters who jumped down my throat the second I messed up when I was growing up didn't exactly make me open to listening to others indicate when I've made a mistake.

"Do we want to go forward?" I hate how weak my voice sounds, but this man makes me weak.

"June Bug," he sighs before kissing my nose, "I haven't made a secret of wanting you back. And yesterday you made me promise to never do a promo stunt with another woman again. I think you want the same thing I do, but you're scared."

I narrow my eyes on him. How dare he say I'm scared? I mean, I am. But, still, who does he think he is mentioning it?

"I'm not scared."

"It's okay, June Bug. I'm scared, too."

Wait. What? "You are?"

He kisses my nose again. "Of course, I am. Relationships are difficult. Add in how I'm away shooting a film half of the year and all the attention the media gives me and you don't exactly have a recipe for an easy relationship."

"True."

"But I'm willing to fight for this relationship. I know how it feels to live without you and I don't want to go back there."

"And you'll communicate with me? Tell me where you are and what you're doing."

His eyes flash with pain before they fall closed and he leans his forehead against mine. "Yes, June Bug, I will. I promise."

I decide to pull up my big girl panties. They're worn and sporting a few holes, but it's the best I can do. "Okay. Let's give this relationship thing a try."

His smile stretches from ear to ear. "Yeah?"

I nod. "Yeah."

He presses his hard length into my core, but I shove him away. "Nope. We don't have time. I need to get to the refuge to check on the animals."

He rolls onto his back with a groan. "Fine. But I am taking you out to breakfast first."

I freeze. "Breakfast? Together?"

"No. I'm going to sit across the room from you." He rolls his eyes. "Yes, together."

I guess we're really doing this. We're going to be a couple. Starting this very moment. Eek!

When we enter the diner thirty minutes later holding hands, cheers erupt from the crowd.

Mav leans close to whisper in my ear, "Are people exchanging money?"

"Yep. Welcome to Winter Falls. We claim to be famous for being carbon neutral when in actuality we should be famous for the amount of betting going on in town. Gamblers Anonymous would have a field day here."

"Juniper!" The diner owner, Gracious, bounds out of the kitchen and engulfs me in a hug. She sways me back and forth. "Thank you for coming to the diner as your first couple outing."

I groan. "How much did you win?"

"I'll never tell." She winks before turning to Mav. "Welcome home, Rickie."

His eyes bug out when she tackles him with a hug. He pats her back. Geez. He reminds me of my sister, Lilac, when she receives public affection. I grab his hand and draw him away.

"Let's get a booth."

Once we're seated at the table furthest from the door, Mav takes a breath. "Is everyone going to call me Rickie now?"

"You don't like having a nickname?"

He shrugs and glances away. "I don't know. I've never had one before. My parents always just called me Maverick."

Sage peers around the back of our booth. "You can't expect us to call you Maverick when the tourists are in town."

Gracious arrives and slaps two menus down on the table. "Leave 'em be, Sage."

"I wasn't the one who tackled him when he walked through the door," Sage mumbles before returning her attention to her own table.

"Now, I don't have any of that fancy oat milk or caramel stuff for your coffee, but I can—"

"Normal coffee's fine," Mav cuts her off to say.

"And I don't need to ask Juniper Berry what kind of coffee she wants," she says as she pours two cups for us.

"Hot and strong is all I need," I murmur before taking a sip.

"I'll let you have some time to—"

Gracious' words are cut off by a scream. An honest to good-ness scream. I pull out my phone intent on calling Lyric to ask him to come to the diner while I search the room for the source of the emergency. My gaze catches on a group of teenagers standing in the doorway of the diner.

"He's here! It's Maverick Langston!"

They rush into the diner before anyone can stop them.

"I knew I recognized the falls on his Insta post."

"It's a good thing your parents dragged you to this Podunk town for vacation last year."

"You should have believed me when I told you the waterfall was in Winter Falls. We could have been here last night instead of traipsing all over Colorado."

"It wasn't all over Colorado."

They stop chattering once they reach our table.

"Hi, Maverick," the first girl breathes out and bats her eye-lashes at him.

I giggle and expect Mav to laugh as well, but he flashes her his Hollywood smile instead.

"What can I do for you ladies today?"

"Can I get a selfie with you?"

"Naturally, darling." He stands and walks away without a word to me.

What the hell? Is he ignoring me?

As I wait and watch and seethe, he takes selfie after selfie with the girls. Once the pictures are finished, the autograph signing begins.

"Do you want us to chase them out of town?" I startle at Sage's question.

"What?"

"Chase them out of town," she repeats.

"I thought no one knew he was here. Do you think someone told?"

"They said something about a picture on the Insta," Clove answers as she sits down across from me in Mav's spot.

I frown. Mav's spot? He hasn't sat there for at least fifteen minutes while he attends to his fans. This is supposed to be our first meal together as a couple. Some couple we are.

"What's the Insta?" Feather asks as she joins us.

"Shouldn't you be serving ice cream?" I ask her.

She shrugs. "No more than Clove should be serving coffee or Sage should be at the police department."

Sage checks her watch. "My shift doesn't begin for another fifteen minutes."

"The Insta is social media," Clove answers Feather's earlier question and I raise my eyebrow at her. "What? *Clove's Coffee Corner* has an Instagram account."

"Uh oh."

I frown at Sage. "Uh oh what? How can this get any worse?"

She points outside the window where another group of young women are rushing down the street. "Come on." She stands. "Let's chase them out of town. This should be fun." She marches out of the diner with Feather and Clove on her heels.

I should help, but I can't leave Mav on his own. I scan the room to discover him laughing and joking it up with the teenagers. I guess I won't be leaving him on his own after all.

I follow the gossip gals out of the diner where they're confronting the women.

"What are you doing here?" Sage asks.

"We know Maverick Langston is in town."

Sage scratches her neck. "Who?"

"Never mind, you old bat. You wouldn't understand."

Old bat? I hurry forward to defend Sage, but I don't make it.

"Who you calling an old bat?" Petal asks and throws her purse on the ground. "I'll show you who's an old bat." She raises her fists. "Or are you afraid to fight?"

What in the name of Eostre is going on? Petal doesn't fight people. No one in this town does. We're lovers, not fighters.

"I respect the elderly. I don't fight them."

Elderly? Oh shit. I push my way through the gathering crowd intent on separating the two.

"Who are you calling—"

Petal's husband, Orion, swoops in and lifts his wife before carrying her away. "I've got her, Lyric."

Lyric appears in the middle of the crowd. "Settle down, everyone. There's nothing to see here."

The locals begin to disperse now the excitement's over. I make certain Sage and Feather are safe before I flee the scene. I don't bother returning to the diner. There's nothing for me there. The last thing I need to witness is Maverick getting all loved up by his fans while he totally ignores me. No thanks.

And here I thought he'd changed. That he was going to treat me as a partner and not a plaything. Stupid me. You'd think I'd know better by now.

Where are you?

I snort at the message. Seriously? It's been over an hour since I left the diner, and he didn't realize I was gone until now? Way to make me feel important.

Work

I'll be there in five minutes

Yeah, no. If I see him now, I'm going to scream and yell at him until I end up saying words I can't take back.

I need space

The phone rings almost immediately. I hit ignore and a message pops up a few seconds later.

Space? Wasn't it you in my arms this morning?

And wasn't it him who totally forgot about me for over an hour while we were supposed to be having our first meal in public together?

When I don't respond quick enough, he tries again.

You said you wanted to try with me.

That was before I realized I meant nothing to him. Not a dirty little secret my ass.

I may have jumped the gun. Please, give me space.

Fine. I'll give you space. For now.

Thank you.

I switch off my phone and wipe my eyes. I don't have time for crying about what a complete idiot I am. I need to care for these animals. At least, they need me.

Chapter 20

I prefer my dog over humans. My dog never asks stupid questions.

"SHE MUST BE HERE somewhere." I hear Aspen say in my living room, and I groan before burying my head under my pillow. I have no desire to deal with my sisters now. Truth be told, I hardly ever want to deal with my interfering siblings lately.

"Found her!" Ashlyn shouts as she dives onto my bed.

Bark Twain and Indiana Bones growl at her before leaping from the bed and rushing off. "Bye, fur monsters."

I throw a pillow at her. "They're not monsters. You're the monster for breaking into my house."

She rolls her eyes. "There was no breaking involved. We used a key." She waves a key at me.

What the hell? She gave me back her key. I should have known she had more than one.

"I'm afraid it's still considered breaking and entering as our entry was unauthorized," Lilac explains.

"But we didn't use any force," Ashlyn argues.

"Did you push the door open?"

Before Ashlyn can respond, Ellery enters my bedroom. "Are we having a slumber party? Awesome." She grabs the pillow Ashlyn's hugging before climbing into bed with me. "Wake me up when you've got Juniper sorted."

"Some help you are," Aspen grumbles as she sits on the floor next to my bed. Indiana Bones returns and lays his chin in her lap.

"Help? Why would I need help? What happened?"

"You missed it." Ashlyn bounces on the bed, and Ellery kicks her. "The town was overwhelmed by Maverick's teenaged fans."

"Teenyboppers," Aspen corrects.

Ashlyn claps. "Excellent. Today will forever be known as the Invasion of the Teenyboppers. Make a note of it," she orders Lilac.

Lilac frowns. "I'll be sure to do that tomorrow."

"Whoa hoo!" Ashlyn throws her arms in the air in celebration. "Lilac used sarcasm."

Ellery groans. "Great. Now, can you reconvene this conversation in the living room so I can get some sleep?"

"This is my bed, you know," I point out.

"I know." She sniffs my pillow. "And guessing by the smell of this pillow, you didn't spend last night alone."

"Give me that." Ashlyn snatches the pillow from Ellery. "I don't smell anything."

Ellery taps her nose. "It's the benefit of having a baby. Apparently, I can smell better than a bear now."

"The African elephant actually has the best sense of smell in the animal kingdom," I tell her.

"And there is no scientific evidence to suggest pregnancy has an effect on olfaction." Lilac frowns. "Although, there are plenty of anecdotal accounts and research in this area is lacking."

"Let me smell." Aspen snags the pillow from Ashlyn and sniffs it. "Oh, yeah. I'm definitely smelling cologne."

"Yes!" Ashlyn punches her hand in the air. "This confirms the rumors from the gossip gals about Mav and Juniper being a couple."

"What's this about the invasion of teenyboppers?" I ask before they can begin grilling me about last night.

"I can't believe you missed it. Weren't you at the diner with Maverick this morning?" Ashlyn asks.

"I had to rush off to take care of my animals," I lie. It's happened often enough for the lie to sound believable. Some what.

Ashlyn's too caught up in the story to question my words. "Apparently, a whole bunch of teenagers figured out Maverick Langston is in Winter Falls, and they invaded the town and accosted him."

"Accosted him? Did they hurt him?"

He didn't appear hurt when I left. No, he seemed perfectly happy to bask in their adoration. I knew I shouldn't get involved with a movie star. What was I thinking? I'm an idiot. No, I'm worse than an idiot. What's worse than an idiot? A nincompoop? A feral cat that refuses to be potty trained?

Ashlyn waves away my question. "He wasn't hurt. No need to worry. I'll bet he can perform just fine." She wags her eyebrows in case I'm confused with what she means by 'perform'. I'm not.

"How did they find him anyway?" I ask, although I already know. Stupid man posted a picture of the falls on social media. What did he think would happen?

"He posted a picture on social media," Aspen confirms my theory.

Ellery yawns and rolls over. "I saw the post. It didn't mention the location."

"It doesn't have to. If he didn't disable geotagging, anyone with a bit of hacking skills would be able to uncover his location. Don't worry, Juniper," Lilac reassures me, "I can show him how to disable geotagging. Today's incident won't be repeated."

Today's incident won't be repeated, but not for the reasons she's thinking. "I heard the gossip gals confronted the fans," I blurt out in an effort to change the topic of conversation to any matter other than a drawn out discussion of me and Mav.

"I think you've changed the subject enough now. Time for you to tell us what's going on with you and Mav," Aspen announces. Dang. She caught me.

I frown at her. "Who says there's something going on?"

Ashlyn wags her phone at me. "Every single person in town."

I growl. Stupid town Facebook page. As if the townsfolk don't gossip enough, there's also a Facebook page to ensure everyone hears the gossip at lightning speed.

"We went to breakfast together. Big deal." I thought it was a big deal. I thought wrong.

"This pillow says you lie." Ellery holds it up.

"You mean the pillow Bark Twain farted on?"

Ellery gags and throws the pillow on the floor. When I burst out laughing, she sticks her tongue out at me.

"You're cruel."

"How's Honey doing?"

I was planning to train the puppy I gifted to Ellery myself, but the second Cole bought her a house, she insisted I hand the pup over, which meant I missed all the puppy cuddles. Puppy cuddles are the best.

"Enough!" Aspen barks and Indiana Bones howls before dashing out of the room. I wish I could follow him. "Tell us why you're laying in bed feeling sorry for yourself when we know for a fact you were all loved up with Mav this morning."

I glare at her. Aspen's my big sister, but it doesn't mean she's privy to every single thing happening in my life. I'm allowed some privacy, aren't I?

Her eyes soften and she reaches out to squeeze my hand. "I'm not being nosy."

Ashlyn snorts. "I am."

"We're worried about you. We didn't know why you were acting like a grumpasaurus these past months."

"I knew." Ashlyn raises her hand.

Aspen ignores Ashlyn to continue, "But now we know about Maverick, we want you to be happy."

I roll my eyes. "Just because you drank the Kool-Aid doesn't mean the rest of us have to."

"The Kool-Aid is quite yummy," Ellery mumbles into her pillow.

"And spicy," Ashlyn adds.

"Lilac and I are perfectly happy being Kool-Aidless." I motion to Lilac who blushes and glances away. "Have you drank the Kool-Aid, Lilac?"

She squirms. "Of course, not. I don't even understand your metaphor." She's lying. Lilac never squirms and she always looks directly at whoever she's speaking to.

"What Kool-Aid have you been drinking?"

Aspen's hand squeezes mine until I cringe from the pain. "We're not here to discuss Lilac's liaisons. We're here to discuss why you won't give Maverick a chance."

"Yeah." Ashlyn bobs her head in agreement. "I thought you agreed to get over the stupid kiss already."

I pry Aspen's fingers from my hand before shaking it out. My bookish sister has more strength than I realized.

"I did get over the kiss. We even talked about the kiss and how he would handle publicity stunts in the future," I admit.

"Then, what's the problem?" Aspen pushes.

The problem is I'm not a priority in his life, but I have no desire to tell her how stupid I felt this morning when he ignored me for his fans.

"Why don't you let this go?"

"Ha! Have I seriously ever let anything go in my life? I still give this one," she points to Ashlyn, "shit about her spying on Lyric and me when we were teenagers."

Ashlyn groans. "Are you never going to let it go?"

"See?" Aspen winks. "I never let anything go."

"If I tell you what's going on, will you leave me alone?"

"Of course."

I point to the mirror above my dresser. "Your fingers are crossed behind your back."

She shrugs. "It was worth a try."

"You might as well tell her or we'll be here all night," Lilac says.

"I know." I sigh. "Fine. Mav and I agreed to begin a relationship this morning."

"Yeah!" Ashlyn cheers.

"Not so quick." Her hands fall and she motions for me to continue. "When those fans came, he left our table and went with them without a backward glance. I waited fifteen minutes and he ignored me the whole time. It was embarrassing." I grab a pillow and bury my face in it.

"Okay." Ashlyn rolls off the bed. "I understand."

I lift my head. She does?

"Wait!" Aspen shouts and Ellery grunts next to me. "You're done? No more questions? No more interrogation?"

"Yep."

Aspen stares at Ashlyn for a moment before nodding. Great. They're concocting some scheme. Leave me out of it. I'll hide out at the Wildlife Refuge until I figure out what to do about Mav. It's not like I can think about anything else anyway.

"Are we done here?" Lilac asks but doesn't wait for an answer before stalking out of my bedroom.

Ashlyn and Aspen link arms before following her.

"Wait!" I shout after them. "Aren't you going to take Ellery with you?"

"Leave her be," Aspen shouts back. "Cole said she hasn't been sleeping well. He'll be happy to hear she's getting some rest."

"Why does her rest have to be in my bed?" I ask but my front door slams and they're gone.

Whatever. I roll to my side away from Ellery. I hope she doesn't snore.

Chapter 21

"I'M HERE!" ASHLYN DECLARES when I give in and open the door after her insistent knocking.

I'm surprised she didn't break in the way she usually does. Of course, there's a small chance – slight really – I told her I still have my snake and I don't know where Slinky is. A little white lie never hurt anyone.

"Why are you here?"

"Duh. To continue our pursuit of the Mystery of the Black Hat Bandit's Missing Loot."

I should probably kick her out. The last thing I want to be doing is scampering around town chasing some imaginary treasure. But what other option do I have? Spending the day moping around my home analyzing every single thing Mav has ever done while trying to figure out if I can play second fiddle in his life?

True to his word, he's given me space. Oh, he hasn't ignored me completely. He sent me a text before I went to bed last night and another one wishing me a good day this morning. Talk about mixed messages! Acting all sweet after ignoring me? My head is spinning.

"The last time we pursued the mystery we ended up committing burglary," I remind her.

She bounces on her toes. "I know. Wasn't it a blast?"

My baby sister is the only person in the world who gets excited about breaking into someone's house. But I do admit I could use something to think about besides Mav and his fans. See what I mean? I'm obsessing. Too bad realizing I'm obsessing can't get me to actually stop with the obsessing.

"Did you figure out the clue?"

Her nose scrunches. "No. But I have an idea."

I open the door further and motion her in. "Come in."

Her eyes scan the floor as she tiptoes into my living room. I bite my tongue to stop myself from bursting out laughing at her obvious fear.

"Have a seat and we can discuss our next step."

"Um. I don't need to sit. I already know our next step."

"Which is?"

"We should go talk to Old Man Mercury."

I rear back. "Old Man Mercury? He's a hermit who'd rather shoot first than ask you questions. Never mind let you in his house."

Slight exaggeration as no one in Winter Falls would dare own a weapon. The fighting when the police force started to carry weapons is the stuff of legends.

"Poor Mercury. He's misunderstood."

"And his house is haunted. Or did you forget the séance we did in his front yard when we were in high school?"

She rolls her eyes. "We didn't manage to connect with any ghosts."

I plop down on my chair, and she screeches. "Be careful!"

"Careful of what?" I dig into the cushions as if I'm searching for something.

"Slinky! He could be anywhere. I'll wait for you outside." She runs out the door, and I burst into laughter. I'm so not telling her the snake is gone.

I give my fur babies some treats before I follow her out of the house and climb into her golf cart.

"What makes you think Old Man Mercury can help us?" I ask as she switches on the engine.

"He knows everything there is to know about Winter Falls."

"I understand Mercury is one of the founding hippies of Winter Falls, but the robbery occurred before the town was founded."

"He's helped before."

Color me surprised. "He has?"

I guess I haven't been paying enough attention to what Ashlyn and Aspen have been up to with this wild goose chase. Speaking of my big sister, "Won't Aspen be mad at you for not including her?"

She dismisses my comment with a flick of her wrist and the golf cart veers to the side of the road. She hits the grass and I grab hold of the dash to stop myself from flying out of the cart.

We bump through the rough ground for a few minutes until she manages to straighten the cart and get us back on the road.

"Oops."

"Does Rowan know you're the worst driver in the history of drivers?"

"Geez. Exaggerate much?"

We manage to reach Old Man Mercury's house without ruining anyone else's lawn, and she pulls up to his porch. While she bounces out of her seat, I don't move. There's a reason Old Man Mercury has the nickname Old Man, although crotchety old man would be more appropriate.

Ashlyn stops when she notices I'm not behind her. "Are you coming?"

"I don't know."

She snorts. "You're okay with snakes slithering around your house, but you're afraid of an old man? You need to get your priorities straight."

I step out of the golf cart. "Because I'm not afraid of an animal, I need my priorities straightened?"

"Snakes aren't animals. They're the devil incarnate."

"Are you two going to stand there gabbing on my steps all day or are you coming inside?" Old Man Mercury barks from the doorway, and I squeal in surprise. When did he come outside? He doesn't wait for us to answer – or my pulse to stop racing – before turning around to march inside his house.

Ashlyn bounces up the stairs and skips along the patio. I sigh before trudging after her. I stand for a moment inside the house allowing my eyes to adjust to the darkness before following her to the kitchen table where Old Man Mercury is waiting for us.

"Where's Aspen?" he yells, and I jump in my seat. Does the man not have an inside voice?

"She's working at the bookstore. We agreed Juniper would join me today," Ashlyn explains as she pours us lemonade.

I wave in greeting.

"How's the Wildlife Refuge going?"

My mouth falls open at his question. How does he know I manage the refuge? The man is practically a recluse. I don't think I've seen him in town for years.

"I'm an old man. I'm not an idiot. I know what's going on in my town."

I clear my throat. "The refuge is going well, thank you. We recently expanded the capybara and fennec fox enclosures. I'm expecting two more llamas this week as well." Everyone thinks llamas are cool to own, but if you don't treat them right, they can be downright nasty.

"You have chupacabras? Aren't you afraid they'll drink the blood of Phoenix's goats?"

Phoenix is Lyric's brother and has a goat farm near the Wildlife Refuge.

"Chupacabras aren't real."

Old Man Mercury snorts. "You just said you have some."

"We have capybaras, giant rodents. Not vampire chupacabras."

"Here I was worried about your snake and you have vampires at the refuge." Ashlyn shivers. "Remind me never to go out there again."

"You haven't been out to the refuge to help since the entire town discovered you're an erotic romance narrator."

"Which reminds me." Old Man Mercury points to a CD on the kitchen counter. "I finished the last book you brought over. Do you have a new one for me? Preferably without too much of BDMS."

I choke on my lemonade and Ashlyn slaps me on the back while asking Mercury, "Do you mean BDSM?"

Holy generic pet food! My choking intensifies until Ashlyn's pounding on my back.

"Stop," I tell her and twist away until she can't reach me.

"What's wrong with you?" Old Man Mercury asks. "Are you a prude? Don't you think old people have sex?"

I grew up in Winter Falls. I'm intimately acquainted with old people having sex.

"Sorry. You surprised me is all."

He leans back in his chair and grunts. "Uh-huh."

"We have another clue, but we can't figure it out," Ashlyn says when the silence becomes awkward.

"Why didn't you say so in the first place? What's the clue?"

"It says – you'll find the item where the steel stops and families reunite. Steel and families reuniting makes me think of a railroad, but Winter Falls doesn't have a railroad."

Mercury grins. "Maybe not, but Winter Creek had one."

"Winter Creek was the settlement before Winter Falls was founded," Ashlyn explains to me.

"Where was the railroad?" I ask.

He points to a towering pile of books on a table next to an armchair. "Grab me the top book, would you?"

When I fetch the book for him, I realize it's an atlas. One of those old-fashioned book ones. I set it on the table and Mercury pages through it until he finds what he's looking for.

He taps the page, which is a map of the state of Colorado. "The railroad ran through the state this way." He traces a finger from the east of the state to Denver. The line he indicates passes near Winter Falls but not through it.

"I can't quite remember when the railroad stopped. It was a long time ago."

"Do you think the railroad was still in use in 1955 when the Black Hat Bandit robbed the Hastings National Bank?"

He scratches the stubble on his chin. "I imagine so."

Ashlyn and I stand and lean over the table to study the map. "I wonder where the nearest stop was," I murmur as I stare at it.

"It was here." Mercury points to a location about ten miles out of town. "There was a small settlement there when we arrived in the state. We considered establishing our community nearby, but people were opposed to the railroad."

"What's wrong with a railroad?" Ashlyn asks.

"What's wrong with a railroad?" Mercury booms as he shakes his head at her. "Don't let your mom hear you ask that."

"I won't."

"The idea of Winter Falls was to grow all our needs locally. A railroad isn't local."

"The railroad station must have been where Robert and Patricia were supposed to meet."

Ashlyn sighs like the tale is some great love story. As if. Their story is not what romance legends are made of. Tragedy is more like it. Robert was a bank robber and Patricia knew it, which is probably why her family disapproved of the union. Unfortunately, Patricia died in a train wreck and the two were never reunited.

"Are there any remnants of the station left?" I ask, although I don't believe there is. The place is ten miles from Winter Falls. Someone would have noticed an old railroad building by now. And since no one in this town can keep a secret, we'd know about it. But this is all news to me.

"You'll have to go figure it out." Mercury slams the atlas closed. "It's time for my nap."

"That's his way of saying he's tired and wants us to leave," Ashlyn whispers.

We say our goodbyes before piling into the golf cart for the trip back to my house.

"This is exciting! We're one step closer to finding the loot."

"For all you know, whatever you find will be another clue."

"I'm not worried. I'll figure it out." She shrugs. "You can't tell me you didn't have fun today. This is an adventure!"

I wouldn't exactly label visiting an old man an adventure, but the whole episode did take my mind off Mav and his forgetful ways for an hour, and for that, I'm thankful. As if I can conjure him with my mind, my phone beeps with a message.

Just wanted to let you know I'm thinking of you

Too bad you forgot I existed when your adoring fans were swooning all over you.

Chapter 22

Animals – unlike humans – know life is to be enjoyed.

"Welcome, West sisters," Ashlyn screams before running full tilt toward Lilac and me as we enter the park where she's having her wedding party.

"I think our mother is going to regret using her power of guilt to persuade Ashlyn to have a wedding party," Lilac murmurs to me.

Saying Mom was unhappy when Rowan let it slip that he and Ashlyn went to Vegas to get married is the understatement of the year. Even Dad got in on the action and guilt-tripped his youngest daughter about wanting to escort her down the aisle. And, thus, today's wedding party was born.

"Mom knew what she was getting herself into."

Lilac raises an eyebrow. "You think our other mother knew Ashlyn would set up a bouncy castle and beer pong?"

"Don't forget the candy land station." I gesture toward the booth sporting a cotton candy machine as well as rows and rows of candy.

Ashlyn nearly rams into us as she reaches us. Someone's been in the candy. "Wow. I'm fast in my running shoes." She lifts her dress to show off her shoes which are indeed running shoes with the word bride written on them in sparkly paint.

"The gossip gals let me borrow their fabric paint."

"What did they want in return?" Because those women know how to negotiate every situation in their favor.

"A bit of juicy information is all."

"Does Rowan know you told them about your sex life?"

"Pfft. What he doesn't know won't hurt him."

"Is this a wedding party or a carnival?" Aspen asks as she joins our group.

Ashlyn throws her arms in the air. "It's a wedding carnival!"

"Someone needs to stop feeding her candy," Aspen mumbles.

"Actually, it's a myth that sugar causes hyperactivity. Over a dozen studies have been conducted and none of them prove any connection between sugar and super-hyperactivity."

Ashlyn does a slow clap. "Thank you to our resident nerd for making a carnival sound boring."

Lilac isn't offended by being dubbed a nerd. "You know this isn't what Mom had in mind when she insisted you have a wedding party."

Ellery joins us while holding little Willow in her arms, and all talk of nerds and wedding parties is forgotten.

Aspen holds out her arms. "Give me my niece."

"Nope!" Ashlyn elbows Aspen out of the way. "I'm Willow's favorite aunt. I've got her."

"Gee. It's lovely to see you, too," Ellery says as she passes her daughter to Ashlyn.

Ashlyn dashes off with the baby. "I've got her, Jeeves. Let's make a run for it."

Cole arrives and throws his arm around Ellery. "Is Ashlyn stealing our baby?" He frowns as he watches Ashlyn and Rowan cuddle his baby girl.

Ellery isn't worried. "She'll bring her back when her diaper needs changing."

"Who thought Ashlyn would turn her wedding party into a carnival?" Ellery asks as she surveys the various games set up in the park.

"Who thinks Ashlyn rigged all the games so she can win today?" I ask before raising my hand.

"How do you rig a beanbag toss?" Aspen asks.

Tap. Tap. Tap. Rowan raps his finger against the microphone, and we turn our attention to the stage where he and Ashlyn are standing.

Cole rushes on the stage and holds his arms out for his daughter. Ashlyn shakes her head and backs away. His hands fist as he follows her. Uh oh, Ashlyn has awakened the gentle giant.

"Give Cole my baby!" Ellery yells.

Rowan glances over and notices the commotion. He sighs before marching to the pair. He removes Willow from Ashlyn's arms before placing her in Cole's. When she pouts and stomps her foot, he leans close to whisper in her ear. She practically melts at whatever he's saying.

He places an arm around her waist and draws her to the microphone.

"Welcome to our wedding carnival!"

At Ashlyn's announcement, the crowd cheers.

"Only my daughter would hold a wedding carnival," Mom complains as she and dad join us.

"I believe she's our daughter," Dad insists. "I distinctly remember helping to make her."

"Ew. Dad." Aspen makes a face.

"It's time for the cake smash!"

Mom's brow wrinkles. "Please tell me she means the cutting of the cake."

"I don't think she does," I sing as I point to the two cakes set up side by side where a crowd is already gathering.

Lilac frowns as she studies the cakes. "What's the goal here?"

"I'm betting on making a mess."

"You can't bet on making a mess. Of course, they'll make a mess," Sage calls from her spot behind me. "The bets are as follows – Ashlyn tackles Rowan. Rowan throws the entire cake at Ashlyn—"

"Never gonna happen," I interrupt to say.

"Ashlyn throws her entire cake at Rowan," Sage continues. Now, that's what I'd put my money on.

Ashlyn's best friend, Moon, arrives with a chalkboard sign and places it behind the couple. I giggle as I read it.

On one side, it states: Rowan Hansley, Age: 31, Weight: 225, Likes: Football, Dislikes: Illegal tackles, Loves: Dream Girl.

On the other side, it states: Ashlyn Dream West-Hansley, Age: 24, Weight: None of your business, Likes: Games she can win, Dislikes: Manipulative Ex-Wives, Loves: Jeeves.

The photographer, Soleil, arrives. Soleil is a Jill of all trades. During the summer, she conducts pottery workshops for tourists. In the slow months, she works at Ellery's bed and breakfast. She also knits vibrator covers and sells them online.

We watch as Ashlyn and Rowan pose for a bunch of pictures. Correction – Rowan poses and Ashlyn goofs off. She sticks out her tongue, makes obscene gestures with her hands, flaps her arms like a duck – you name it, my baby sister is doing it.

"Ahem." Mom's had it. "Can my youngest daughter pretend to be an adult for a few minutes? I want to have at least one nice picture of today."

"A picture of me pinching Rowan's epic ass isn't nice?"

"Let me pinch his ass, Ashlyn, and I'll fight in your corner," Feather calls.

I glance over at her and notice the group of gossip gals all standing together. They're wearing bright, prink t-shirts with the words *Gossip Gal Wedding Helper* on them.

"If someone's pinching Rowan's ass, it's me," Petal argues. Her husband grunts next to her but doesn't bother arguing. He's not a stupid man.

"I've babysat, Rowan. I've seen his naked ass." Sage crosses her arms over her chest to indicate the argument's over.

"It's not the same if he was a baby," Clove argues.

"Besides," Cayenne adds, "I've seen his ass in my yoga class. His adult ass."

"Hold up!" Ashlyn raises her hands and waves them around to gain everyone's attention. "Since when does Rowan do yoga?"

No one has a chance to answer before Forest shouts, "Stop!" as he dashes across the park. I'm happy to note he's wearing pants today because men and running naked do not mix. "I said stop!"

Is he talking to us? Does he want in on the pinching Rowan's ass contest? It's not really a contest. Rowan's not letting anyone but his wife pinch his ass.

"Juniper, help!"

Son of a dog. There's only one reason Forest would ask for my help. I rush to the front of the crowd and scan the ground. There he is. Chip is dashing toward the tables where the cakes are laid out – his gaze fixated on the baked treats. His front paws lift off the ground and I move to block him. He springs into the air and I snatch him before he lands on the table.

"Gotcha!"

With Chip secured in my arms, I start toward Forest to return his pet to him, but I miss the leash dangling from the chipmunk's neck and my foot catches on it. I teeter and place a hand on the table behind me to catch my balance. While I'm trying to steady myself, Chip decides to use my chest as a springboard to escape. The pressure of his jump forces me back into the table.

The table rocks and I snatch my hand away before it can tip over. I wheel my arms in an attempt to balance myself, but it's no use. I fall backwards and crash into the table. The table collapses and I topple to the ground. Before I have a chance to orientate myself, the first cake crashes down on my head. The second cake isn't far behind it.

I wipe cake and frosting from my eyes until I can see. My dress is completely covered in frosting and chocolate. Maybe being blind was better.

"Oh no. I'm sorry, Ashlyn," Forest yells his apology as he continues to fight to control Chip.

Ashlyn bursts out laughing. "This turned out better than I could have ever imagined. Someone please tell me you got pictures."

Aspen holds up her phone. "I recorded the entire incident. I'll upload it to the Facebook page now."

I spring to my feet. "You are not putting a video of me being attacked by cake on Facebook."

"Wanna bet?" She holds my gaze as she pushes a button on her phone. "Done!"

I launch myself at her. Lyric pushes her behind him before I can reach her.

An arm catches me around my waist. "Stop."

I freeze at the sound of Mav's voice.

"Who invited Maverick freaking Langston to this party?"

"I did." Ashlyn raises her hand.

"You little shit."

She wags her finger at me. "Nuh-uh. No name calling. I'm the bride. I'm queen for the day."

"At least that explains why she's wearing a crown, although I'm confused as to why it's a big top," Mav murmurs from behind me, and I shiver at the feel of his breath on my skin. *No! There will be no shivering!*

"I guess I'll settle for smacking down my big sister," I declare before I lose what's left of my mind and lean into Mav's hard body.

Aspen peeks out from behind Lyric.

"Chicken!"

She responds by sticking out her tongue at me.

I struggle in Mav's arms, but he doesn't let me go. "Come on." He throws me over his shoulder. "Let's go get you cleaned up."

Applause breaks out from the crowd. "You go get her, Rickie!"

I hear someone ask, "Did anyone bet on Juniper destroying both cakes?"

I pause in my attempt to escape. This is too embarrassing. I should hide instead. And since Mav is marching away from the party, I'll hide my face against his back. It has nothing to do with enjoying the strength he displays when carrying me. Nope. Nothing at all.

Chapter 23

MAVERICK

I dump Juniper in my bathroom. "Get cleaned up. We'll talk when you're done."

"Talk? We don't have time. I need to get back to my sister's party." Her voice is reaching panic levels by the time she finishes.

I cock an eyebrow. "You do?"

She plants her hands on her hips and her breasts jut out. I force my gaze to remain above her neck. Now is not the time to act like a horny teenager, although being in Juniper's presence makes me feel like one.

"It's her wedding party. Of course, I do."

I shake my phone at her. "I guess it wasn't your sister who sent me this message telling me to – and I quote here – 'don't let Juniper escape'."

"Returning to the party isn't escaping," she argues, but her shoulders fall forward in defeat.

I cup her chin in my hand. "Time's up, June Bug."

She straightens her shoulders. There's my girl. Never down for long. "I have no idea what you're talking about."

"I let you have your play. I gave you time to think. Time's up."

I don't let her respond. I plant a hard kiss on her mouth before exiting the bathroom.

I dig around in my drawers and find a t-shirt and sweatpants that will fit her if she rolls up the bottom of the sweats. I wait until I hear the water in the shower flowing before entering the bathroom and placing the items on the vanity.

"I laid out clothes for you," I tell her as I shut the door behind me.

I pace in the living room as I wait for her to clean up. I didn't lie to Juniper. Her time is up. I gave her space to think about us. Whatever the hell space is supposed to mean. I have no idea what crawled up her ass. She was perfectly happy in my arms in the morning and the next thing I know she disappeared on me.

I hear the bedroom door open and bare feet pad toward me. When I glance Juniper's way, I have to stop myself from rushing her. Her silky hair is wet and hangs down her back. The t-shirt I lent her is too small in the chest area and her perky breasts strain against the material. Something deeply possessive stirs to life in me at the sight of her in *my* clothes in *my* house.

I fist my hands and lock my knees before I say to hell with talking and herd her into my bedroom where I can worship every inch of her body. Later, I promise myself.

"May I return to Ashlyn and Rowan's party now?" She grits out between clenched teeth.

"Hold up. Are you mad at me? I brought you here to clean up."

"No. You carried me here against my will."

"Against your will?" I growl. "I have never, nor will I ever, do anything to you or any other woman against their will."

She sighs. "I'm sorry. You're right. That was a shitty thing for me to say."

I nod in acceptance of her apology.

"But I would like to return to the party."

"After," I tell her.

"After what? I'm no longer covered in cake and frosting. I can change into another outfit at my house. It's not as if it matters what I'm wearing. Ashlyn's throwing a wedding carnival for goodness sakes."

"After we talk things through."

Her eyes close and her chin falls to her chest. "I'm not ready."

"Too bad. You yelled at me – rightfully so – for not communicating with you and made me promise to communicate better in the future. Communication is a two-way street."

"I hate it when you point out my mistakes," she grumps.

"We all make mistakes," I say and motion to the couch. "Let's sit."

She takes a seat on the couch as far away from me as possible. I let her. I can't imagine having a serious conversation with her in my arms. I can barely think when she's near. When my hands are touching her, forget about thinking. My thoughts are on one-track and one-track only then.

"Why did you say you need space?"

"You're not going to build up to the big question first?"

"What would you like to talk about first? How you tried saving the wedding cakes from a chipmunk and ended up covered in cake?"

She salutes me. "Touché."

Silence falls and I wait her out. Juniper may be stubborn as the day is long, but she's also impatient. She'll give in eventually.

"Fine, I'll tell you!" She throws her hands in the air. "You forgot I existed the minute your fans showed up."

"I—" I start, but she doesn't let me get a word in.

"It was supposed to be our first outing as a couple, and we didn't even have the chance to order before you were ignoring my existence. You didn't bother to glance back as you trotted off with your adoring fans."

"It's not how it looked," I manage to say while she catches her breath.

She ignores me to continue her rant. "Here I thought we were starting over. That you weren't going to ignore me for all your Hollywood glitz and glamour. I'm such a fool."

I've had enough with the pain obvious in her eyes. I scoot down the couch and grasp her hands.

"You're not a fool, and I don't give a shit about the Hollywood glitz and glamour."

She snorts. "Which is why you ran to your fans the second they showed up in Winter Falls."

I lift her until she's straddling me and cradle her face in my hands. "I didn't want them to know about you."

She rears back and nearly tumbles off my lap. "What? Are you ashamed of me? Am I not good enough for you?"

She fights against my hold, but I'm not letting her go. Not when I finally have her right where she belongs.

"No. You're too good for me."

"If I'm too good for you, why are you hiding me like I'm some dirty little secret?"

"I'm trying to protect you." She frowns and I rush on. "Once the paparazzi know about you, they'll dig into your life and invade your privacy."

She slaps my shoulder. "You need to stop making decisions for me. I know the paparazzi will dig into my life and guess what? They won't find anything interesting. I don't have a sordid past they can uncover. There are no old boyfriends with grudges waiting for the chance to air our dirty laundry. I'm boring."

I kiss her nose before placing my forehead against hers. "You, my June Bug, are anything but boring. You also told me about the night you spent in jail. Do you know what the bloodsuckers will do with that piece of juicy information?"

She smirks. "Good thing they'll never find out about it."

"Jail records are public."

"There is no record. Lyric was the officer who caught us with the 'rocket fuel' and he never made an incident report, but he did make us stay the night in jail to 'teach us a lesson'." She makes air quotes as she rolls her eyes.

"Are you positive you want the world to know about us? Once the cat's out of the bag, there's no putting it back in." I need her to understand how difficult things can get.

"Tell me about it. I love my Meowise, but she is a total asshole."

"I'm serious, June Bug. Reporters will overrun Winter Falls. It'll be a shit show."

"It's cute you think the press will get anywhere near Winter Falls."

"You can't stop them. They're relentless."

"In which case, it's a good thing my sister knows how to hack, isn't it?"

I file away this tidbit of useful information for later and continue to push, "You're absolutely positive you want to join the circus?"

Her eyes sparkle with amusement. "Have you met my family? My sister is literally having a wedding circus as we speak." When I don't appear convinced, she cradles my face in her hands. "I'm positive."

"I love you." I don't give her a chance to respond to my declaration before crashing my lips on hers. She immediately opens to me, and my tongue seeks hers out as we duel for supremacy. I let her play for a while before taking over and dominating the kiss.

When my need to breathe overwhelms me, I release her lips. My fingers curl into her hair and I tilt her head back. As she gasps for air, I trail kisses along her neck until I reach her ear where I bite down on the lobe. She moans and grinds down on me.

"Why are you wearing clothes?" She pouts as she tears at my jeans.

I shackle her wrists. "I'm not having sex with you on my couch."

"Why not? Is this a rule you have? Because we're going to have problems. I love couch sex."

I nod toward the window. "I need to put up blinds before we have sex in the living room."

"In that case …" She bounces to her feet and holds out her hand. "Let's move our activities to the bedroom."

I grasp her hand and allow her to drag me toward the hallway. She glances back at me over her shoulder and smiles. "By the way, I love you, too."

Her words hit my heart and my chest warms. The warmth spreads through my body until I'm ready to burst with happiness. This is why I worked my ass off to get a second chance with her. I knew it'd be worth it.

Chapter 24

Mav's arm tightens around my waist as I inch toward the edge of the bed. "Where are you going?" He snuggles up to my back. "I had plans for this morning."

I groan when he rolls his hips and his hard length hits my back. "I don't have a choice."

"Are you sure?" His hand dips under my t-shirt before skimming along my skin until he reaches my breast. His finger traces circles around my nipple, and I moan before arching into his hand. His other hand cups me.

"I guess I'm going to be late," I gasp out.

"Excellent." He re-arranges us until he's looming over me. He grasps the edge of my t-shirt and I lift my arms. He whips the material off of me and ... my phone rings.

"Ignore it," he orders when I reach for it.

"I can't. The animals, my family. Something could be wrong."

He snatches my phone off the bedside table and passes it to me before rolling off and stalking toward the attached bathroom. Unlike me, he slept completely naked, and I can't help myself from watching his glorious backside as he leaves.

"Hello! Hello!" Lilac yells into the phone.

"I'm here."

"No, you're not."

Mav shuts the door and I'm able to concentrate on the conversation. "What do you mean? I'm talking to you on the phone, aren't I?"

She huffs. "I'm at your house and you aren't here."

"Why are—" I cut myself off and swear under my breath when I remember she was supposed to pick me up this morning.

"Go along to Ashlyn's without me. I'm going to be late."

"I'll wait for you. I'm fifteen minutes early."

Of course, she is. "I'll be there in five," I say and ring off.

I throw on the clothes Mav lent me yesterday. "I'll see you later," I shout toward the bathroom before dashing out of the room.

He catches me at the front door. "Use my bike," he says before kissing my cheek. "When will you be home?"

Home? Does he mean his house or mine? "I don't know."

"Just let me know. I'm reading scripts all day, but I'm available if you need me."

I stare at him. This is such a normal conversation about our everyday lives. We've never had one of those before. I'm not certain how to react.

Mav smirks as he pushes me out of the house. "You're late, remember?"

With a whole lot of breakneck pedaling and the fastest shower in the history of womankind, Lilac and I manage to arrive at Ashlyn and Rowan's house a mere ten minutes late.

I'm still catching my breath when Ashlyn bounces her way toward me. She taps her chin and studies me for a few moments before announcing, "Juniper got herself some last night."

I'm not going to deny it. I can't. I think I spotted a hickey Mav gave me on my neck while I was showering. So much for keeping a low profile.

"You're one to talk. You're practically glowing from the sex vibes emanating from you."

"I assume she's glowing due to the increased amounts of hormones being released in her body because of her pregnancy."

At Lilac's words, everyone freezes. I feel my jaw drop.

"It's true. Project Get Ashlyn Pregnant is a success!" Ashlyn is yelling by the time she finishes her announcement.

My mouth gapes open and closed several times before I manage to get my brain to form words in a coherent manner. "No wonder you chose a wedding carnival. No one could question you not drinking."

"Sneaky smart, right?"

I pull her in my arms. "I'm happy for you, baby cakes."

She shoves me away. "No. No more calling me baby cakes. You can't call me a baby when I'm having a baby."

Aspen hugs her before announcing, "You'll always be baby cakes to me."

Ellery sniffles before wrapping her arms around Ashlyn. "I'm so excited. Our children will grow up together."

"If Ashlyn's child is as wild as she was, you better put aside money for bail now."

Ashlyn rolls her eyes. "Our children's uncle would never arrest his niece and nephew. I want a boy. An adorable boy who looks exactly like Rowan."

"You better stock up on condoms early," I mutter.

"Don't worry. I got this covered. Although, I won't be giving my child the sex talk at the age of six." Ashlyn makes a face at the memory of those sex talks our mother subjected us to.

I hear a crash and whirl around to discover Mom standing in the foyer. The cake she brought is in pieces at her feet. "Child? You're pregnant?"

"I prefer the term knocked up."

While Mom and Ashlyn giggle and embrace, I get out the broom and sweep the remnants of the cake away.

"This must be familiar to you," Aspen says.

"What?"

"Picking up cake." She wags her phone at me. "At last count, the video had 155,000 views."

"What? You weren't supposed to put the video online for everyone to watch." It's bad enough every resident of Winter Falls will see it.

"I made no promises."

I drop the broom and stomp toward her.

"Now, now, baby girls." Mom pushes her way between us. "No fighting. Today is a happy day. I'm going to be a grandmother."

"Ahem." Ellery clears her throat. "You already are a grandmother, remember?"

"Yes. Yes. Of course. Speaking of which, where is my little Willow today?"

"Cole took her fishing. As if a five-week-old baby is interested in learning how to fish."

"Can we start opening presents now? I have to work today."

I frown at Lilac. "It's Sunday. You shouldn't be working on Sunday."

"Unless she's working on one of her liaisons." Aspen wiggles her eyebrows.

Lilac purses her lips. "Do not focus your matchmaking schemes on me. I am perfectly happy the way I am. Now, presents."

"Presents!" Ashlyn screams at the top of her lungs and runs off.

"Are we supposed to follow her?" Lilac asks as she watches Ashlyn skip down the hallway.

I shrug before trailing my baby sister down the hall to her study. I gasp when I notice the sheer amount of presents piled high on every available surface including the floor.

"Holy cow. Did every single person in Winter Falls send you a present?"

No wonder she asked us to help her open presents today. I thought she wanted witnesses to watch her tear into her gifts. I didn't realize she seriously needed help.

"Rowan's former football team found out about the marriage and they all sent presents."

Aspen smiles as she enters the room. "Wow. I can't wait to get married."

"Too bad your future husband isn't a football god," Ashlyn teases.

"Nope. He's the Chief of Police meaning everyone is going to send a present to court favors."

Lilac sighs. "You do realize the situation you're describing is bribery."

Aspen shrugs. "I'm not a police officer. They can't bribe me."

"I need to make a phone call. I'm going to be late." Lilac pulls her phone out of her purse before leaving the room to find privacy to make her call. Silly woman. Privacy doesn't exist when you have four sisters. She should know better by now.

Ashlyn tiptoes after her. I'm right on her heels. Our sister, the person I'm convinced isn't one-hundred percent human, is keeping secrets and I need to know what they are.

"I'm afraid I'll be delayed." Naturally, Lilac doesn't greet the caller first. She sighs as she listens to his response. "I'm sorry, Beckett, but there's nothing I can do."

Oh, Beckett. Sexy name.

"No, I will not leave my sister's party because we need to complete work we could have easily finished on Friday had you told me it was required on Monday morning."

Lilac sounds frustrated. She's never frustrated. I widen my eyes in Ashlyn's direction and she nods. She heard it, too.

"Fine. We will discuss this tomorrow."

Lilac growls as she ends the call and throws her phone in her bag. Suddenly, I understand Aspen's obsession with match-making. This is going to be fun.

"Come on." Ashlyn laces her arm through mine. "You can tell us all about what happened after Maverick carted you off from my party yesterday."

Did I say fun? I misspoke.

"How about it's none of your business?"

She giggles. "Nice try, but no dice. I want all the juicy details."

"I'm not giving you any juicy details. You never tell us juicy details about Rowan."

"You have to at least tell us how you went from crying in your bed about him to spending the night in his house," Aspen insists.

"I wasn't crying in my bed. Besides, how did you know I spent the night in his house?"

She waves toward Lilac.

"Tattletale."

Lilac shrugs. "You didn't tell me it was confidential and swear me to secrecy."

Robot Lilac strikes again. She doesn't believe in lying. She'll do it, but you have to warn her in advance and fill out a form – in triplicate. I'm exaggerating but not by much.

"Fine," I hiss and proceed to tell them about the discussion Mav and I had.

Aspen claps when I finish. "This is wonderful. I'm so win-ning the bet this time."

I don't bother asking her what bet she's talking about. This town will bet on any and everything – including what color your underwear is. Don't ask.

"Can we please move on to opening Ashlyn's wedding presents now? We're going to be here all day as it is."

"Presents!" Ashlyn shouts and dives onto the pile.

I sag in relief as everyone turns their gaze from me to watch my baby sister's antics.

Chapter 25

If you're going to talk to an animal, listen to what it has to say.

"What is Beltane anyway?"

At Mav's question, I stop on the sidewalk. "Sometimes I forget you don't know much about Winter Falls."

He taps my nose. "But I'm learning."

He is and I love him all the more for it. It's been a week of bliss since Ashlyn's wedding carnival. I never thought I was the kind of person to use a word such as bliss, but there's no other word to describe how wonderful it's been being with Mav in a real way.

No more sneaking around. No more lying to my family about where I've been or who I've been with. Plus, Mav's been a great help at the Wildlife Refuge. My typical twelve-hour days have become normal eight-hour workdays. Bliss, I tell you.

"Beltane is the celebration of the peak of spring and the coming summer. The name Beltane is derivative from Belenus, the Celtic sun god." I clear my throat before admitting to the rest. "It's strongly associated with fertility."

He cocks a brow. "Fertility?"

I feel my face heat up. "As in there are fertility rituals."

He places his hands on my shoulders and leans forward to meet my gaze. "Do you want children, June Bug?"

I shrug. "Maybe in the future. I'm only twenty-six."

"Your sister's twenty-four and she's pregnant."

"My sister also chased after the man she loved for years until she wore him down and then she promptly decided she was going to give him a baby as soon as possible. No one should make decisions based on what Ashlyn does."

"And Ellery just had a baby."

I cock my head and study him. "Are you trying to say you want children?"

"Would it be such a bad thing to have my babies? The baby would be conceived in love since I love you and you love me."

My heart seizes and I forget how to breathe. Maverick Langston, movie star and Hollywood A-lister, wants to have children with me?

He rubs my neck. "Relax, June Bug. I don't want to lay you down on the grass at this very moment and plant a baby in you. Although, if you want to go back home, I'm down with practicing."

I wag my finger at him. "Don't distract me. I'm in the middle of a meltdown."

"Why? Are you not open to having children?"

I throw my arms in the air. "I don't know! I've never thought about raising the next generation of Hollywood legends."

He frowns. "Who said anything about Hollywood legends? This is just me and you, Maverick and Juniper, talking about having children in the future. Hollywood has nothing to do with it."

I blow out a breath before nodding. "You're right. I freaked out there for a second. Can we erase the last three minutes from the record, please?"

He smirks. "And lose the opportunity to remind you of how you had a meltdown at the idea of having my children? No way."

I punch his shoulder. "You're adapting to Winter Falls entirely too well."

He throws an arm over my shoulder, and we begin making our way toward the town square again. "Now, tell me all about these fertility rituals. Will there be naked men running around tempting the women of town?"

I giggle. "You have some weird ideas about fertility rituals."

"And I've spent a fair amount of time in Winter Falls. Naked men running around wouldn't be very unusual."

He's got me there. I lean into his shoulder as we walk. "Thank you."

"Thank you for what? Being awesome? You're welcome."

I tickle his ribs and he swats my hand away. "No. Thank you for letting the subject of our future children drop when it freaked me out."

"Of course, June Bug. I know it's early in our relationship to discuss children, but I thought I'd put it out there."

"I'm not opposed to having children, but I don't want to rush into parenthood the way Ashlyn and Ellery did." Although Ellery's foray into motherhood was a complete accident.

"Understood," he murmurs before kissing my hair.

We continue on for a few minutes in silence until we reach the town square where the Beltane festival is happening.

"What are those?" Mav asks indicating the bonfires.

"Those are bonfires."

"I'm sorry, but those are not bonfires. For one, there's no fire."

"The candles simulate fire," I argue even though he's right.

There are no bonfires on Beltane in Winter Falls despite the traditional use of bonfires for the festival. Bonfires are bad for the environment and Winter Falls is tolerant of many things, but not of anything harming the earth. Thus, the towers of candles instead of bonfires. Truth be told, the majority of the candles aren't lit either.

"What's with the goats?"

"According to tradition, cattle would be passed between the two fires to purify them and ensure the fertility of the herd."

"I may be a city boy, but I'm fairly certain cattle and goats are not the same species."

I giggle. "You would be correct, but there are no cattle farms in Winter Falls – and please don't ask me why – thus, the goats."

"Why can't I ask why? Is there something nefarious about …" Mav's questions drop off when he notices Phoenix passing by with two of his goats on leashes.

"Is he going to walk the goats between the two candle fires?"

Phoenix hears and answers for himself. "Yes, I am. I'm going to walk my goats on leashes between the two candle towers.

Afterwards, I'm going home and drinking a whiskey and pretending I don't own leashes for my goats."

"Someone's grumpy," I sing.

"Someone was up all night with a sick kid."

"Why didn't you ring me?" I'm not a vet, but considering my experience with wild animals, I often help Phoenix out when he's having issues with his animals whether it's the goats or the chickens or the rabbits.

"I was ordered not to bother you."

I snort. "Since when do you listen to orders?"

"Since they threatened I'd be the next person to be matched if I didn't leave you alone."

There's no doubt who 'they' are. "You know they're going to try to match Lilac first."

"Can't chance it, Juniper. I can't chance it."

"Why not?" I ask, but he's already moving his goats away. I nearly follow him to dig further, but I know what it feels like when everyone's up in your business. I'll give him his privacy. For now.

"I think you need to interpret your conversation for me," Mav says when we're alone again.

I pat his arm. "The only thing you need to understand is the gossip gals are on my shit list."

He shivers. "I'd be careful if I were you."

I roll my eyes. "Don't tell me you're afraid of a bunch of old women."

"Who you calling old?" Cayenne barks from behind me, and I lock my muscles to stop myself from jumping and screaming.

I fist my hands on my hips and go on the attack. "You shouldn't have—"

I don't have a chance to finish my accusation before Sage rushes toward me and begins hauling me away. "Come on. Come on. It's time for the maypole dance. You don't want to miss an entire year of fertility, do you?"

I plant my feet. "As a matter of fact."

I look up at Mav with pleading eyes. I may even pout my bottom lip a bit. Didn't he agree to save me from fertility rituals today?

He places an arm around my waist and hauls me near. "What's this about a maypole dance?"

I indicate the giant pole in the middle of the square. There are several ribbons in a variety of colors attached to the top. Several women, including three of my sisters, grasp the ends of the ribbons.

"No time to explain," Sage grunts out as she continues to try and drag me away. "It's starting."

"Why do women dance around the maypole and not men? After all, both the male and the female must be fertile in order to produce a child."

"He's not wrong," Rowan says as he joins our group.

"I'm all for it, but Aspen kicked me when I took hold of a ribbon," Lyric adds.

"You'd think in a town that prides itself on equality both the men and the women would be involved in any fertility ritual," Cole adds. Baby Willow waves from the carrier on his chest as if she agrees.

"Maybe we should kick off a new tradition. The men and the women will dance around the maypole," Mav suggests, and I give him the stink eye. So much for helping me avoid the fertility rituals today.

"About damn time," Forest booms as he comes up to us. "I've been saying the maypole dance should be inclusive for years."

"What do you say, June Bug? You want to dance around the maypole with me?"

Dang it. If Mav is willing to dance around the maypole, I can hardly say no.

"Will someone snap some photos?" I'm going to need evidence for future bribing purposes.

"I got this," Sage says and holds up her camera.

I narrow my eyes on her. She was awful quick to agree to this. She winks at me. Shit. She planned this all along, didn't she? How the hell did she manage it?

Mav entwines his fingers with mine. "Come along, June Bug. It's time to celebrate spring or the coming of summer or fertility or this god Beltane or something similar."

I laugh as we hurry to the maypole with Cole, Lyric, and Rowan on our heels. "I'm impressed with how close you listened to my explanation."

I wave to Aspen, Ellery, and Ashlyn as we pick out ribbons to hold onto. "Where's Lilac?"

Aspen points to one of the bonfires. "Pretending to be fire marshal."

"She's full of bologna," Ashlyn shouts. "She's afraid of the maypole."

"Having a baby isn't a horrible thing. In fact, it's pretty awesome," Ellery adds as she smiles at Willow.

"I can't wait," Ashlyn says as she stares up at Rowan with her hand on her belly.

The entire town is going to know she's pregnant if she doesn't stop rubbing her belly. Of course, knowing Ashlyn, she won't care if everyone knows before it's 'proper' to tell people. She doesn't do proper.

The first strains of *Zombie* by the Cranberries begins and everyone starts dancing.

"What is this?" Mav asks. "I thought we'd dance to some Gaelic folklore music."

"In Winter Falls?" I have to yell to be heard over the music.

He tilts his head back and laughs. It's a beautiful sight. One I hope to witness every day for the rest of my life. I am so gone for this man. If he leaves me, I'll be lost with no desire to be found.

Chapter 26

The difference between a house and a home is a four-legged creature.

"Do you want to bike over to my place later or shall I wait for you to shower?" Mav asks when he drops me off at my house.

To my delight, he showed up to help at the Wildlife Refuge today. Despite being terrified of the capybaras – a fear I don't bother to hide my amusement of – he's quite helpful. The llamas have really bonded with him, although I did have to remind him llamas are not horses. You can't ride them. You'll break their poor spines.

I scrunch up my nose as I consider his question. "Why don't we stay here?"

I love Mav's house, but we're always at his place. Despite how much time we've spent there in the past weeks, the place still doesn't have the feel of a lived-in home whereas my house is definitely lived in. It's comfy to a fault.

"Do you not like my house?"

I am not answering his question. "Do you not like mine?" He frowns. "What about my animals? My poor dogs are feeling orphaned."

He can't argue with me there. Bark Twain and Indiana Bones have spent entirely too much time alone lately.

He motions to my entrance. "Lead the way."

I open the door and lock my knees in preparation for the canine assault except no assault comes. "Bark Twain. Indiana Bones. Where are you?"

Meowise lifts her head from the sofa where she's lounging and promptly gives me her backside. I'm not surprised my cat's annoyed with me. She may ignore me for the most part when I'm home, but she does want me to be home. She wants me to notice she's ignoring me, dang it.

I go in search of my dogs. The first place I look I hit gold. They're laying on my bed as if they own it. "Hey, my sweet things. How are you?"

Indiana Bones ignores me completely, and Bark Twain yips before farting. I fan my face as the odor hits me.

"What does he eat?" I ask myself as I crawl onto the bed to give them some loving. I need a few minutes and lots of belly rubs before my fur babies cuddle into me, and I know I'm forgiven.

Mav enters the bedroom and contemplates the bed. "You need a bigger bed."

I waggle my eyebrows at him. "Afraid you can't get the job done in a smaller bed?"

"Challenge accepted." He prowls toward me but stops when his gaze snags on my terrarium. His Adam's apple bobs as he stares at it. "Why do you have a terrarium?"

"It's for Slinky."

"S–s–slinky?"

"Yeah, Slinky the snake."

He inches backward. "There's no snake in there."

"No, there isn't."

He's in the hallway by now. "Where's the snake, Juniper?"

I shrug, because technically I don't know where Slinky is at this exact moment.

"Where's the snake, Juniper?" He screeches his question this time.

I bite my lip as I study him. How far should I push this little joke of mine? I bet I could get him to run out of the house like his pants are on fire. I should probably act as if I'm a grown-up, though. Sigh. Being a grown-up is boring sometimes.

"Slinky isn't here."

"You're certain he isn't around here somewhere?" Mav's gaze skitters over the floor.

"You got ants in your pants?" He's bouncing from foot to foot and his face is reaching nuclear level red.

"Tell me where the snake is!"

I roll off the bed and approach him with my palms out. "It's okay, Mav. The snake isn't here. I promise you."

"Promise?" His voice is two octaves higher than normal. Someday I'm going to tease the living shit out of him for it, but today is not that day.

I grasp his hands and squeeze. "Yes, I promise."

His shoulders fall and he blows out a puff of air. "I hate snakes."

I raise an eyebrow. "You don't say."

"I was bit by one when I was filming *Romancing the Writer.* They didn't know if the snake was poisonous or not and I had to be airlifted to the nearest hospital, which was a three-hour helicopter ride away. The entire time I thought I was going to die in some no name hospital in a no name town on the edge of a jungle in South America."

I wrap my arms around him. "I'm sorry. No more snake jokes."

"And maybe you could get rid of the terrarium?"

"Because you asked nicely, I will." I release him to pick up the glass enclosure. "I'll put it in the garage for now. I can probably sell it back to Forest."

"Forest?" he asks as he opens the door to my garage for me.

"He owns the pet store, *Unleashed,* remember? He's the man who thinks wearing pants should be optional."

He groans. "Now, I remember. The man has no shame."

I set the terrarium on a shelf. "From what I've seen, there's nothing for him to be ashamed of."

"Juniper Berry West, have you been checking out Forest?"

I shrug. "He's kind of hard to miss."

"He's old enough to be your grandfather."

"And, according to my mom, love is love and we shouldn't judge other people if they want to have a dalliance with an older man."

He chuckles. "Dalliance?"

"Do you prefer the word sexual relations? Or intercourse? Maybe coitus? I swear coitus was my mom's favorite word when we were growing up."

"You mom talked to you about coitus?"

"Didn't your mom ever give you the sex talk?"

He snorts. "Um, no. Moms do not give sons the sex talk."

"I didn't expect a man who's danced around the maypole to be such a sexist."

"It's not about being sexist. It's about knowing how the parts work from first-hand experience," he explains as he shuts the garage door, and we return to my house.

"The parts work? What parts are we talking about?"

"I don't think I can tell you." I raise an eyebrow. "I need to show you." He presses his hard cock into my back.

"I might need to examine how these so-called parts work in order to understand."

He leans down to lick the skin behind my ear. "I think I can arrange a demonstration," he whispers, and goosebumps break out on my skin.

I glance over my shoulder and flutter my eyelashes at him. "What about my parts? Do you want to examine those?"

He skims a finger along my shoulder. "I think I would."

"You'll have to catch me first," I say and rush off toward the bedroom.

The dogs bark and give chase, as does Mav. I nearly make it to my bathroom when an arm wraps around my middle. "Gotcha!"

He lifts me up and throws me on the bed like I weigh nothing. I mean, I'm skinny, but his strength in throwing me is sexy as all get out.

I bounce on the mattress and the dogs bark before springing onto the bed after me. I shove them off, but they merely jump back on again as if we're playing a game.

"This is ridiculous," Mav complains before grabbing Bark Twain and carrying him out of the bedroom. He shuts the door on him before returning for Indiana Bones. Indiana Bones isn't about to be pushed around, though. He runs around the bedroom and Mav chases after him until I finally have pity on him.

"Indiana Bones," I yell. My baby immediately halts and stares up at me with those puppy dog eyes. I wag a finger at him. "Don't give me the look. You know you're not allowed in the bedroom when I have a male visitor."

He drops his head and his tail curls under his body as he trots to the door. Mav opens it and Bark Twain immediately sticks his snout in the room. Mav wrestles with the dogs but eventually manages to force them out into the hallway and shut the door on them.

"At least, Meowise didn't try to join the fun. She's a scrapper. I'd hate to have to treat your wounds."

Mav ignores my comment as he climbs onto the bed and covers me with his body. "Now, where were we?"

His lips slam down on mine before I have a chance to answer. Who needs to answer? The answer is my tongue searching his out. Our tongues barely have a chance to touch before the doorbell rings. Mav wrenches his lips from mine with a scowl.

"I'm going to kill whoever's at the door," I grumble.

"Unfortunately, you can't. It's our food."

"Food? There aren't any delivery services in Winter Falls." Delivery services are bad for the environment. Don't ask. Just accept the statement, unless you want to hear an hour-long lecture complete with PowerPoint presentation.

"I asked Moon to bring us some hamburgers from the brewery."

I shove him off of me. "Go. Hamburgers from the brewery need to be eaten warm."

"This will be continued later."

"Of course. Of course. Food now. Sexy times later."

As I watch him saunter out of the room, I debate whether I made the right choice in picking food first but when the smell of hamburgers and fries hits me, I know I definitely made the right choice. Besides, Mav isn't going anywhere. He's in Winter Falls to stay.

Chapter 27

Whoever said cats are angels with fur forgot about the beady eyes and hissing.

MAVERICK

"You must be Ricky Ricardo." Ashlyn winks as she opens the door to *Bertie's Recording Studio,* the recording studio she owns in 'downtown' Winter Falls. 'Downtown' as in it's on Main Street, the one and only shopping street in town.

"Sorry," I tell her. "Old habit."

I haven't checked into a hotel or made a dinner reservation under my own name in more than a decade. I learned the fast way restaurant maître d's and hotel receptionists will sell you out for twenty bucks without blinking an eye.

"No worries. I figured you wanted to keep your visit on the down-low." She gestures toward the floor.

"Are you making jazz hands at the floor?"

She sticks her tongue out at me before asking, "Want me to show you around?"

"You seem full of energy considering your condition."

"My condition? What century are we living in? Victorian England where saying the word pregnant is considered gauche?"

"I thought your pregnancy was secret. I didn't want to say the p-word in case anyone overheard me."

She throws out her arms and twirls around. "There's no one here. You can say whatever you want. You can scream bloody murder, and no one will hear you."

I feel a surge of protection. "Isn't it dangerous meeting new clients by yourself? You should be more careful."

She blows a raspberry. "Are you going to join the 'Ashlyn can't do anything by herself because she's pregnant' group? Because I have to tell you, there's not enough bubble wrap in the world to keep me contained."

"You appear to be feeling well," I say instead of touching her comment. I know better than to go overprotective on a West woman. The lot of them are stubborn and independent to the nth degree.

"I'm feeling great. Apparently, I'm one of the lucky few who don't experience morning sickness." She skips in a circle around the reception area. "But don't tell Ellery. She'll be super jealous. She was sick during most of her pregnancy." She halts. "Wait. You can tell Ellery. She's allowed to be jealous of me."

"Sibling rivalry. I'll never understand it." Although I've witnessed it more often than I'd prefer to in Hollywood. All those reality star families appear to have wonderful loving relationships on-screen. Off-screen, it's a different story.

"Do you not have any siblings?"

"You don't know my entire background? You seem the kind of person to conduct a background check on everyone. If only to use the information you dig up as blackmail material later."

"I'm not much of a blackmailer. If someone does me wrong, I prefer to paint a clown face on them while they're sleeping and post it on social media."

"Remind me never to give you a key to my house."

"As if I need a key." She smirks. "Anyway, Lilac's the sister who conducts background checks on people."

I wasn't actually being serious. "How does she manage it? Is she a private investigator as well as an environmental engineer?"

She giggles. "You're funny. Lilac, a private investigator? Ha! Considering PIs are usually hired by husbands to discover who their wives are sleeping with, I think we can safely say Lilac is not a PI."

"Hey! Husbands cheat on their wives, too."

She bursts out laughing, bending over and holding her belly, for such a long time I worry she's going to hyperventilate, which can't be good for the baby.

"F-f-first you get all the men to dance around the may-pole—"

"Hey! It was Cole's idea to join the women. Not mine." Truth be told, it was a blast. I don't think you're supposed to dance around a maypole while listening to rock music, but it worked.

She ignores me. "Afterwards, you insist men have as many infidelity problems as women. You're all about equality. No wonder Juniper loves you." Her eyes widen, and she slaps a hand over her mouth. "Ignore me. I didn't say anything. La. La. La. La."

I debate letting her suffer for a while, but she appears to not be breathing. Rowan will kill me if Ashlyn passes out from holding her breath.

"It's fine. I know Juniper loves me." She raises an eyebrow. "She tells me so herself often enough."

"Yeah!" she shouts and bursts into song. "Love is all around us. The feeling is getting bigger and bigger. Yeah. Yeah. Yeah."

"I don't think those are the lyrics to the song."

"Who cares? My sister's in love, and it's not with an animal."

"I'm fairly certain your sister is still in love with a whole bunch of animals."

She shivers. "You better not be talking about Slinky. Snakes freak me out."

"Agreed. But there's no need to worry about Slinky. He's gone."

"He's what? When? Why that little snake-loving, animal-loving, lying sister of mine! I ought to break into her house and stuff poison ivy in her shorts. That'll teach her."

I motion to the studio. "Maybe we should leave the sister abuse until later. I believe you're supposed to be giving me a tour of the recording studio."

She grunts. "I guess."

Phew. I don't fancy spending the night in the emergency room because Juniper has a rash in all kinds of uncomfortable places.

"This is the reception area."

The area appears to be a comfortable place to hang out with its black, leather sofas.

"This is the kitchen. Rowan didn't originally build a kitchen." She rolls her eyes. "What was he thinking? Recording artists need their drinks. Personally, I prefer tea when I'm recording."

"Juniper told me you're an audiobook narrator."

"I specialize in erotic novels." She waggles her eyebrows. "Let me know if you need me to narrate anything for you. A special message. Something to get you in the mood. I can help."

The last thing I need in this world is the little sister of the woman I love to narrate a sexy message for me. It's the very definition of a turnoff.

"And these are the recording booths. Don't ask me what all the fancy schmancy equipment does. I'm not a producer. But I can tell you it's the best of the best in the business. I have client reviews you can read if you want."

"The recording booths are soundproof?"

"The building is too."

I'm impressed. The studio is top-notch. I know the place has a reputation in the music industry, but I didn't expect a brand new recording studio with top-notch equipment in Winter Falls.

"Now, how can I help you?" Ashlyn plops down on a sofa and motions for me to do the same.

I drum my fingers on the arm of the sofa as I consider how to proceed.

"Are you having second thoughts?"

I decide to be honest. "You're the one who told me you can't keep a secret."

"Ah, I understand your confusion. I will not keep secrets in my capacity as mayor. As a business owner, however, I'm bound by confidentiality. Rowan made me follow a class on business ethics and everything."

"He did?"

"Yeah. He was worried I'd snap pictures and post them on social media if my clients were famous singers or rock bands."

"And have you had any famous clients?"

"Besides yourself? Not a one." Except she won't meet my eyes. Hmm…maybe Ashlyn can keep a secret after all.

I lean forward and plant my elbows on my knees. "Here's the thing. My parents pushed me into the acting gig. I wanted to go in another direction."

"Let me guess. You wanted to be a rockstar."

"Not a rockstar. A singer."

"Can you sing?"

"I sang the theme song for the movie *Romancing the Writer*."

"You did? Not bad, Rickie. Not bad." She snorts a laugh. "Now, I get the Ricky Ricardo reference. Good thinking."

I actually hadn't realized the connection myself. I'm just a big *I Love Lucy* fan. When you end up homeschooled because you're on set four out of five days of the week, you don't have many friends, and television soon becomes your best friend.

"My parents let me continue to follow music lessons as they thought music abilities might come in handy as an actor."

"What instruments do you play?"

"The guitar and the piano."

"We have keyboards available. You're on your own for a guitar, though. Apparently, guitars are similar to vibrators. Musicians are very picky about them."

I cough. Does this woman have no filter at all before words fly out of her mouth? It's refreshing being around someone so obviously genuine.

"I have a few of my guitars here."

"Do you need me to hook you up with a songwriter?"

"You have songwriters on retainer?"

"Not on retainer, but I've made a few friends in the biz."

"And, I hear you have connections with quite a few of my contemporaries."

Ashlyn went to a drama school famous for producing Hollywood stars. From what Juniper's mentioned, she knows quite a few actors.

She waves away my comment. "Not really. Me and Hollywood stars don't have much in common. Except my sister, of course." She picks up a tablet from the table. "Now, let me see when we have openings in the studios. And, then, you can tell me why I need to keep this a secret."

"I never promised to tell you why I want this kept a secret."

"Bummer. I was hoping for some wild story about needing a creative outlet after Juniper scared you by placing a snake in your bed."

I shiver. "You're crazy."

"Thank you."

I book a few hours of booth time before leaving. I'm nearly vibrating in excitement at the idea of spending actual time in a recording studio. When Juniper asked me if I always wanted to be an actor, I didn't have an answer. No one's asked me what *I* wanted in such a long time, I forgot I have a say in the matter. Plus, I've spent the past years suppressing my desire to sing.

There's no reason to continue hiding what I really want. I've made my money. I have no excuse for not exploring other artistic avenues. And I wouldn't be the first Hollywood star to cross over to singing. I can't wait to tell Juniper.

Except. Maybe I'll wait and keep this secret for a bit longer. I don't want her to get her hopes up I'm quitting acting.

I finish putting on my lipstick and step away from the mirror to check out the final product. Who is the sophisticated woman staring back at me? I'm wearing a blue sheath dress that hugs all my curves and high heels I'm certain are going to cause me to trip and break my ankle.

And then there's the make-up. I hardly wear the stuff, to be honest. But now I have the whole smoky eye thing going as well as a ruby red color on my lips. Mav isn't going to recognize me. Here goes nothing.

I make my way into the living room staring at my feet as I go to make sure I don't trip. When Mav gasps, I look up.

His legs eat up the space between us until he's standing in front of me. His eyes flare with heat.

"June Bug, you look beautiful." His gaze drops to my lips and his head descends.

I smack his chest. "No! Do you have any idea how long it took me to get this make-up correct? I watched five – five! – YouTube videos about lipstick. You are not messing it up before we arrive at the restaurant."

He groans before tugging me close and wrapping his arms around me. "I won't ruin your make-up now, June Bug. But later." He pauses to nip my earlobe and I melt into him. "Later, I'm going to worship every inch of your body."

I do a full-body shiver before pushing him away. "Stop. You promised to take me out to a nice place for dinner. I'm holding you to your promise."

"June Bug, you can hold me to the promise of worshipping every inch of your body later, too."

I roll my eyes. "Such a man."

He adjusts himself in his pants. "I'm definitely a man."

"Let me say goodbye to my sweet things and then we can go." I search the living room, but my fur babies are nowhere to be found.

"I already gave them their treats." He points to the kitchen floor where Bark Twain and Indiana Bones are chewing on rawhide bones.

I bend down to pet them goodbye, but my dress stops me before I can come close to touching them. I hope I don't drop anything tonight because anything on the floor is staying there. I can hardly scrunch my dress up to my waist in front of strangers. Not every place in the world is okay with nudity the way Winter Falls is.

"Bye, sweet things," I call, but neither one of them pays me any mind. "I guess I know where I stand in priority in their lives." It's behind bones.

Mav places his hand in the small of my back to lead me out of the house. The material is sheer, and I can feel the heat of his body through the fabric. Suddenly, I don't know why I insisted we go out on our date night. We can have a date night at home. Without clothes.

While I'm fantasizing about Mav taking care of business, he maneuvers me into his car. He kisses my forehead and ensures I'm buckled up before slamming the door and rushing around the front to the driver's seat.

"Are you in a hurry?"

He growls at me. "Have you seen yourself in that dress? We need to get this dinner over before I combust."

I giggle in delight. "And here I wasn't confident about the dress."

"Darling, the dress is perfect. And those shoes…" He clears his throat and switches on the ignition.

The V8 engine rumbles and I forget all the reasons why gasoline engine cars are forbidden in Winter Falls as I snuggle into the butter soft leather seats.

"Did you get dispensation to drive in Winter Falls?"

"Are you afraid Lyric is going to arrest me, and we'll spend the night in jail?"

"One, *we* wouldn't spend the night in jail as you're the one driving. And, two, if you're in jail, I guess I'll have to drive this beast home."

"You can drive my car anytime you want."

I fast blink at his offer. "You'd let me drive your one-hundred-thousand-dollar car?"

He snorts. "The manufacturer suggested retail price on this baby is closer to two-hundred-thousand dollars."

My mouth drops open. "Your car is worth more than my house."

He shrugs. "It's just a car."

"And yet, you'd let me drive it?"

He glances over at me and winks. "If you'd let me, I'd buy you one."

"You're crazy. Certifiable. When was the last time you had a psychological exam?"

"Two years ago."

"Wait. What? You've had a psychological exam? I was joking." I realize I sound like a jerk and start backpedaling. "I'm sorry. I shouldn't make fun of mental problems. I was shocked is all."

His hand lands on my thigh and he squeezes. "It's okay, June Bug. I know you were joking. One of the movies I did required I pass a psych exam before they'd insure me during filming."

"Phew. You're not an ax-wielding psychopath?"

"I am not." He caresses my thigh. "And don't think I don't know you switched the topic of conversation because you're freaked out about driving my car."

"I'm not freaked out about driving your car. I can drive the hell out of this car."

I'm full of shit. I'm twenty-six years old and only have a driver's license because Mom required all of her daughters to get one when we turned eighteen. She insists we be prepared. For what, I don't know, but my mom and preparation are best buds. Thus, the plethora of safe sex talks I endured as a child.

"Then, why are you having a mini freak-out over there?"

I cross my arms over my chest. "I am not having a mini freak-out."

"Uh-huh. And your toe isn't tapping, and your thigh isn't jumping."

"You're supposed to pretend not to notice."

"Sorry." He traces circles on my thigh with his thumb and I nearly forget what we're talking about. I want him to move his hand a bit higher, underneath my skirt. I'm caught between opening my legs to give him room to work or closing them so I can rub my thighs together for a little relief.

"Please tell me what's wrong. I can't fix it if I don't know what's wrong."

His words bring me out of my fantasy where he's laid me across the hood of his car and— I shut those thoughts down. *Stop acting like a hussy, Juniper.* You stop acting like a hussy, I tell my body.

His hand travels from my thigh to caress my cheek. "What's wrong, June Bug?"

With his hand no longer near my core, the fog lifts from my mind. "You said you'd buy me a car worth two-hundred-thousand dollars. Why wouldn't I be freaking out?"

"One, I wouldn't buy you this model. You'd get the hundred-thousand-dollar one."

I slap his shoulder. "You're not funny."

He glances over and winks at me. "Except you're smiling."

"Whatever."

"Second, I love you. I want to spoil you."

I clear my throat. "You know I'm not with you because of your fame and fortune, don't you?"

He chuckles. "Yeah, Juniper, I figured out pretty early on you weren't interested in money when you refused to accept an annual pay raise."

I shrug. "I make enough money to live a comfortable life. I don't need more."

"June Bug, you deserve more. You work harder than anyone I know."

I refuse to engage. We've already had this argument more times than I can count. "Let's agree to disagree."

"Agreed. To recap, I know you're not with me for the money and you know I want to spoil you."

"Can you spoil me by making a larger enclosure for the fennec foxes?"

"I don't think you understand the concept of me spoiling *you* and not your animals."

He slows the car and turns into a driveway. "Where are we?"

"You'll see."

We drive for a few minutes before we arrive at a restaurant. The building sits up high on the side of a hill with views of the mountains beyond.

"This place is gor—" My words cut off when I notice Mav securing a wig over his hair. He's already wearing a fake beard. "What are you doing? Is this a costume party?"

"This is my disguise."

"Disguise? Why do you need a disguise?" I search the parking lot for fans or paparazzi, but the place is empty.

"I don't want anyone to recognize me and ruin our evening."

I squirm in my seat. This is my fault. "I'm sorry I overreacted when those fans discovered you in Winter Falls. I didn't handle your fame very well."

He stops fiddling with the wig. "And now? Do you think you can handle my fame now?"

"I'm going to try. I love you and I don't want to lose you." I blow out a puff of air. "I guess I got complacent living in Winter Falls where everyone considers you Rickie and not Maverick Langston, the movie star."

"As much as I'm your Mav, I'm also Maverick Langston. And I do get recognized in the middle of nowhere restaurants no matter how much I don't want to."

"What happens when you get recognized? Is it always the same as what happened in Winter Falls?"

"It varies. Those were the younger fans. The ones who view me as a sex symbol."

I waggle my eyebrows. "You are pretty sexy."

He tweaks my nose before continuing, "There are also older fans who can be cool. They want to say hi and for the most part, will leave me alone. And, finally, you have the movie buffs who want to discuss every aspect of every film I've ever been in. They can talk my ear off if I let them."

"I never thought about fame as a burden."

"It's not a burden." He's quick to correct. "It's my privilege to have fans who adore me and want to spend time with me."

And I love him all the more for viewing it this way. For not being a snob who thinks he's entitled to fame and fortune and adoring fans.

"I need to know you can handle my fame. I'm in deep with you, June Bug. You're under my skin and I never want to let you go."

My stomach warms at his words. "I feel the same way."

"Good. Because if you can't deal with this part of who I am, it'll gut me."

The vulnerable look in his eyes has me rushing to reassure him. "I'll do my best. I can't promise to never get annoyed or mad, but I'll try to not be a jealous girlfriend who runs away at the first hurdle."

I did that already. It only caused the both of us pain.

He leans across the console to touch my lips. "Now we've settled the issue, let's go eat. The sooner I get you fed, the sooner I can get you home and talk you out of your dress."

He won't have to work very hard at it.

"Let's go."

Chapter 29

All I'm saying is the canary was alive before you got here.

"Knock! Knock!" Ashlyn shouts before walking into my house.

I cock my eyebrow. "Are you sure you want to be in here?"

She fists her hands at her hips. "Yes, because I'm positive someone lied to me about a certain snake and its whereabouts."

There's only one way she could know the truth. "Mav told you?"

"Yup."

When did Mav and Ashlyn meet without me? According to him, he's been spending all of his time at home reading scripts to decide the next movie he wants to act in. Is he lying to me? *Whoa, Juniper.* What are you thinking? Do not go down the rabbit hole. Step away from the edge. You are not the jealous girlfriend. Moving on.

"What's up? What are you doing here?"

"I can't stop by my sister's house for a visit?"

I snort. "When have you ever stopped by anyone's house for a visit without having an ulterior motive?"

"You make me sound like a supervillain." She beams. "Thanks."

"You don't want to be a superhero?"

Her nose wrinkles. "Of course, not. Superheroes are boring. Always saving the world. Bah. The villains are the interesting ones. They come up with fantastic inventions and are out for revenge."

Why did I ask? I should have known Ashlyn prefers villains to heroes, although she is married to her own real-life hero. Rowan can do no wrong in her eyes.

Speaking of Rowan… "How's the baby?"

She rubs a hand over her still flat belly. "Mini-me is doing great. Doesn't let me sleep much, but otherwise, you won't hear me complaining. Make sure you mention it to Ellery. Ashlyn's pregnancy is way easier than hers was."

"I'll phone her right now."

She wags her finger at me. "No need to be sarcastic. You, too, can get pregnant and have a mini-me."

Except I don't want a mini-me. I want a mini-Mav complete with piercing blue eyes and thick brown hair. *Hold up, Juniper.* You're not ready for children, remember? Exactly. No mini-Mavericks. Yet.

"Did you stop by to convince me to join the pregnant brigade?"

"Nope." She pops the p but says no more. I don't wait her out. It's a toss up as to which of us is the most stubborn, although Ellery will always win most stubborn West sister of the century.

"But you came here because…"

She rocks on her heels. "Because I figured out the next clue in the Mystery of the Black Hat Bandit's Missing Loot!" She raises her arms in the air and whoops.

"And it is …"

"Can't tell you. I have to show you." She motions toward the door. "Time to go."

"Slow down, little missy. You're pregnant. You should be concentrating on growing your baby and not chasing after some loot, which probably doesn't exist in the first place."

She shoves her hand in my face. "Nope. I will not listen to my sister tell me what I can and cannot do as a pregnant woman. Rowan's bad enough. Slow down. Don't jump off the stairs. Don't light the kitchen on fire. Geez. I'm having a child. I'm not a child."

"You set the kitchen on fire?"

She waves away my concern. "It was an accident. Who knew you're not supposed to put aluminum foil in the microwave?"

"Literally everyone in the entire world knows not to put metal in a microwave."

She rolls her eyes. "Obviously not every single person as I didn't know."

"What were you doing putting aluminum foil in the microwave anyway?"

"I was making Rice Krispie treats."

Her answer doesn't clear up my confusion. "What does aluminum foil have to do with Rice Krispie treats? And doesn't your husband own a bakery? If you want sweet treats, he can bake them for you."

"It was supposed to be a surprise. He'd see the treats and be all 'Ashlyn, you're the best wife in the world, let me show me how much I love you in the bedroom'."

I cough to cover up my laugh. "And that isn't what happened?"

She huffs. "He came home, and the microwave was very slightly – seriously, it was hardly noticeable – on fire and he didn't even notice my brand-new negligee."

I can't hold my laughter in any longer. "Only baby cakes can ruin a seduction by accidentally starting a fire."

She pokes a finger at me. "No calling me baby cakes. We've discussed this."

I wipe tears of laughter from my eyes. "Whatever you say, baby cakes."

"Having sisters sucks sometimes," she grumbles. "Do you want to come with me to solve the mystery or not?"

I consider telling her no, but I'm honestly afraid of what kind of trouble she'll get into by herself.

I motion to the door. "Lead the way."

"Don't you need to love up your gazillion animals for an hour before you can leave?"

"Nope. Let's go," I claim, but as soon as she's not looking, I kneel down and give both my dogs a rub down. "Be good, sweet things."

"A car?" I ask when I notice the vehicle in my driveway.

"I know how to drive."

"You do? I was there when you failed your driver's test."

"The examiner had it out for me."

"Uh-huh. Sure, he did."

"He did! No one else has to parallel park and do a three-point turn during their test."

"Are you serious? Everyone has to know how to parallel park and do a three-point turn to pass."

"Whatever. Hop in."

"Show me your driver's license first."

She sticks her tongue out instead and climbs in the driver's seat.

"Where are we going?" I ask once we're on the road.

"To the railroad station a few miles north of town."

"I thought the station wasn't there anymore."

"It's not."

"Then, why are we going there?"

"You'll see," she sings before increasing the volume on the radio and effectively cutting off any further conversation.

I sit back and wait. Ashlyn always brings the entertainment. She might drive me to the brink of sanity, but she's always entertaining.

She pulls to the side of the road fifteen minutes later. When she climbs out of the car, I follow her.

"What am I supposed to be looking at?"

"Hold on," she says as she opens the trunk to reveal a shovel and trowel. Someone came prepared. "Can you carry those?"

"Did you bring me as the muscle?" I ask as I remove the two tools.

She slams the trunk. What she doesn't do is answer me, which means the answer is yes.

"Follow me."

She trudges through the overgrown grass until she reaches a copse of trees. "This is it."

"I'm confused as to what 'it' is. I don't see any railroad tracks and I certainly don't see a railroad station."

She points to a line of trees. "Those trees are much younger than the other ones."

I squint as I study them. "You're right."

"I'm fairly certain the railroad was here. Plus, I found some old railroad ties over there."

"Just how much time have you spent out here searching for the next clue?"

"Enough."

"Does Rowan know what you're up to?"

"No. And you're not telling him either. He's turned into an overprotective maniac. He's not the owner of me."

"Maybe not, but he is the father of your baby."

"I know. Which is why you'll be doing the digging."

Great. I am the hired help.

"I'm not digging up the entire state of Colorado. For all we know, the bandit hid the money in a locker in the train station. A train station that no longer exists."

"I don't think he did."

This is going to be good. "Why not?"

"I can't tell you. I have to show you." She marches off and I follow her. She indicates an area free of trees. "As far as I can tell, this is where the station was. I searched the area but whoever removed the station must have gotten rid of the foundation as well. The only indication there is of a station ever being here is the lack of trees."

"The townspeople of Winter Falls would not have let a building go to rot. They would have recycled the materials." Winter Falls gives more than lip service to the idea of saving the environment.

"I thought the same. I also thought about the previous clue. It was buried in the ground. Maybe the bandit buried this clue in the ground, too."

I open my arms wide to indicate the amount of ground there is to cover. "But where?"

"Since the bandit carved into the foundation of the old mansion, I thought maybe he'd carve into a tree."

"There are an awful lot of trees here."

"There are. But there's only one tree with the initials PH and RA carved into it with a heart surrounding them."

PH as in Patricia Hall and RA as in Robert Adams? My jaw drops open. "No way. You found a tree with those carvings?"

Her smile stretches from ear to ear. "I did."

This, I've got to see. I motion her forward. "Lead the way."

"I told you this is an adventure," she shouts as she runs toward a tree. "It's here. Do you see it?"

I kneel down and lo and behold there it is – a carving with the initials of the black hat bandit, Robert Adams, and his lover, Patricia Hall.

"What are you waiting for? Get to digging."

I remove my sweatshirt and lay it on the ground before tying my hair up in a ponytail. "I hope you brought drinks and food. This may take some time."

Fortunately, I'm used to digging and my work at the Wildlife Refuge keeps me in good shape. Even so, I've sweated through my t-shirt within fifteen minutes. I wipe a hand along my brow.

"Here." Ashlyn shoves a bottle of water at me. "You need to keep hydrated."

I drink half the bottle in one go before stretching my back muscles from side to side. "If I don't find anything within the next fifteen minutes, we're going to have to fetch help."

"You'll find something," is Ashlyn's immediate answer.

"Uh-huh. I'm sure your belief has nothing to do with not wanting to confess to Rowan what you've been up to."

"I hate how much you understand me."

"You love me, and you know it. It's why I'm the baby's godmother."

"I never asked you to be the baby's godmother."

"But you will," I claim before beginning to dig again. The shovel hits something hard and the reverberation has me clenching my teeth.

Ashlyn drops down to her knees next to the hole before picking up the trowel. "What is it? What did you find?"

"It's probably a tree root. Don't you dare go digging now."

I wrench the trowel from her and kneel next to her. I use the small shovel to dig around the hard patch. Once I've managed to free up the area, I tap where it's hard and it makes a clanging sound.

"That is definitely not a root," Ashlyn shrieks.

I dig until a metal lockbox is revealed. "This better not be another clue," I grumble as I lift the box out of the hole and set it on the ground next to Ashlyn who's now holding a pair of wire cutters.

"This is it. I can feel it." She cuts the lock and flings the box open. Her eyes widen when she sees what's inside. "Yowzah!"

I'm speechless. I can't believe it. The box is filled with cash. I grab a stack of bills to be certain I'm not hallucinating after all the hard work I performed, but the paper in my hand is real. Old and brittle but real.

"We found it. We freaking found it." Saying the words out loud doesn't make it seem any more real.

"We found the loot and solved the mystery of the Black Hat Bandit's Missing Loot," Ashlyn screams into the sky.

I fall down on my behind next to the box. This is unbelievable.

Chapter 30

When I first meet an animal, I say hello. When I first meet a person, I avoid eye contact.

MAVERICK

Juniper squeezes my hand to stop me before we can enter her parents' house. "Are you sure you can handle Sunday dinner with my family? My family is kind of crazy and don't exactly know what personal boundaries are."

"Nooo, you're joking. A West family member not know what boundaries are?"

"Is he being sarcastic?" Lilac asks as she opens the door.

"And they eavesdrop constantly and give you no space," Juniper grumbles as she glares at her sister.

"You're standing on the front porch. You can hardly claim it's a private location."

Ashlyn rushes forward and claims Juniper. "Good, you're here. We can finally discuss what to do with the loot we discovered."

Juniper growls. She told me all about how Ashlyn wanted to call the press and announce the find. There was no way my June Bug was letting the press descend on Winter Falls. She's way too protective of my anonymity and I couldn't love her more for it.

I trail behind them into the house and wave in greeting to everyone. I guess we're the last to arrive since all of her sisters and their men – except Lilac as she's currently single – are already here.

Contrary to what Juniper thinks and despite my rough start with them, I'm comfortable with her family. Everyone's genuine. And no one is intimidated or impressed by my fame. It's refreshing. And, yes, I realize how often I'm saying the word refreshing lately.

Aspen crosses her arms over her chest and snarls at her baby sister. "I can't believe you finished the mystery without me."

"We discussed this. You agreed," Ashlyn insists.

"I agreed you could ask Juniper for help while she was down in the dumps about this guy." She points to me and mouths *sorry*. "But now they're all loved up and you still asked Juniper to go with you to the old train station where you found the money."

Ashlyn cocks an eyebrow. "Were you going to dig a hole for thirty minutes until we found the box?"

"I could have tried, but you didn't even give me the chance."

"No offense, Aspen, but you're the nerdy bookstore owner. Juniper here is the outdoorsy animal lover whose only requirement for digging the hole was water."

Juniper flexes her biceps for everyone to see. "I could have used a sandwich, though."

"If you're done showing off your brawn, we do need to discuss what to do with the money," Lilac says.

"What does the law say?" I ask Lyric since I have no clue how treasure hunting works in real life despite starring as a treasure hunter in one of my movies.

"It's more complicated than finders keepers," he begins. "If the money they found is considered treasure trove—"

"Which it should be," Lilac interrupts to say. "The money was found hidden and it's old enough for the true owner to have passed away."

"Anyway," Lyric continues as if he's used to being interrupted by Lilac. What am I thinking? He probably is. "It could belong to the finder or the owner of the real property of where the trove was found."

"Who owns the property?" I ask.

Everyone turns to Lilac as if she has all the answers to all the questions.

"The town of Winter Falls purchased the property a decade ago." I guess she does have all the answers.

"In which case, the money should go to the town to support the community center," Juniper states.

"But Mav is already donating the rest of the money we need," Ashlyn protests.

Juniper's nostrils flare as she glares at her sister. "You are not using my boyfriend for his money."

My heart warms and my cock twitches at how vehemently she defends me. No one has ever stood up for me before unless they were being paid to.

"He volunteered."

Juniper gazes up at me. "Still sure you want to hang around with my family?"

"Your family?" Her mom scoffs. "He's our family now, too. Speaking of which, where's your family, Rickie?"

My attempt to not fidget isn't a complete success as Juniper notices and narrows her eyes on her mom. "Mom."

"What?" Mrs. West is all big doe eyes of innocence. I nearly snort at the act. If there's one thing I know about Juniper's mom, it's that she's not innocent. "I need to know if I have to prepare everyone to chase his relatives out of town."

Lyric groans. "Can you not talk about conspiring with the rest of the town when I'm here?"

Aspen sighs. "How many times do I have to explain? When you're in this house, you are not the Chief of Police."

"I'm always the Chief of Police," he claims before leaning close to whisper, "and you enjoy it when I'm in charge."

Ashlyn slams her hands over her ears. "Na na na na. I can't hear you."

"Good. If you can't hear them, then you can't hear me when I say all the money is going to the community center," Juniper declares.

"But I already know what I want to buy," Ashlyn pouts.

"Dream girl, you don't need the money. I'll buy you whatever you want." Rowan pulls her close and kisses her hair.

"I don't want you to think I'm using you for your money."

This conversation sounds familiar.

Rowan winks at her. "Don't worry. I know you're using me for the sex."

Mrs. West clears her throat. "Speaking of which, I know Ashlyn and Rowan don't need any condoms—

"'Cuz I'm knocked up," Ashlyn interjects.

Mrs. West ignores her and points to the front door. "I've put a few boxes of condoms for you near the door." When I don't have an immediate response to her statement – I'm certainly not going to remind her of our earlier discussion about contraception, it was embarrassing enough the first time around – she backtracks. "Unless you want to give me another grandchild. All good things come in threes."

Juniper holds up her hands. "Mav and I aren't ready to have children."

Ellery snorts. "As if being ready to have children is a requirement to getting pregnant."

"Ellie girl," Cole warns.

"What? It's true. I sure as hell wasn't ready."

"I am!" Ashlyn shouts and wakes up Willow who was sleeping in Cole's arm. The tiny bundle lets out a scream that could wake the dead.

Ellery takes the baby from Cole before stomping out of the room while glaring at Ashlyn.

"Sorry," Ashlyn hollers after her.

Cole rubs a hand down his face. "It took two hours of screaming to put her down."

"Have you tried—" Lilac's question is cut off when her phone rings. She purses her lips at the object before walking off to answer it.

Juniper grasps my hand and tugs me along so we can follow her. She places a finger over her lips to shush me and I roll my eyes.

Lilac paces the back deck as she answers the phone. "It's Sunday. I am not coming into work." She inhales through her nostrils in an attempt to calm herself. "Not that it's any of your business, but I'm not on a date. I'm at Sunday dinner with my family." She pulls the phone away from her ear and stares at it. "I swear if he weren't my boss, I'd complain to HR about him."

Ashlyn peeks around the door. "About who? And please give us a physical description."

Lilac frowns at her sister. "Beckett is six-foot-tall and weighs a hundred and eighty-four pounds."

"Strangely specific."

"What did you expect? She probably made him weigh himself for accuracy," Juniper says and they high-five.

"Don't be daft. His weight is in his employee package."

"Lunch is ready," Mrs. West announces, and everyone makes their way to the table.

"Everything looks wonderful, Mrs. West." I'm not lying. The casserole looks and smells delicious. My mom never cooked like this for a family meal. She wasn't the best of cooks to begin with and when I started to earn a decent amount of money, she decided she never needed to cook again.

"It's nothing. And I already told you to call me Ruby. Unless you prefer mom."

"Mom," Juniper whines, "he has a mother."

She sniffs. "It doesn't sound as if his egg donor has earned the privilege to call herself mom."

"You don't know anything about her," Juniper insists.

"I know he flinched when I asked him about his family. I don't need to know anything more."

At her announcement, a hole in my heart I didn't realize existed starts mending itself.

"Thank you, Ruby. I'd be honored to call you mom, but I think my June Bug would have a heart attack if I did." I wink at her, and she giggles and blushes.

"My daughters. I must have done something right with them considering how handsome and smart all their boyfriends are."

"Husband!" Ashlyn corrects.

Aspen can't let her baby sister have the last word. "Fiancé!"

"Mine's a fiancé, too," Ellery adds as she joins us. "I put Willow down in the nursery."

"You can leave her there. I'll bring her to you tomorrow," Ruby states.

"No, Mom, you can't steal my daughter."

Ruby shrugs. "She's my granddaughter."

Juniper squeezes my thigh. "You okay?" She speaks low so no one else can hear her.

"I'm more than okay." I kiss her forehead. "I'm perfect."

And I am. I wasn't exactly worried about the West family accepting me. Except for the first family dinner I crashed, they've been nothing but welcoming since I showed up at Ellery and Cole's surprise engagement party. But hearing Juniper's mom act like a mama bear on my behalf is more than accepting. It's not lip service for them to say I'm part of the family.

I haven't felt part of a family in a long time. My own parents treat me more like a bank than their son. I glance around the table at everyone teasing and play fighting with each other. If Juniper will let me, I'll give her several children so they can grow up this way.

Chapter 31

"HONEY, I'M HOME," I yell when I enter Mav's house.

I'm not actually home. I haven't moved in with Mav, although I do spend most of my time at his place. Much to my dogs' dismay.

When he doesn't answer my greeting, I go to find him. I don't have to search long. If he isn't in front of the television 'screening' movies – because apparently, you can't simply watch a movie if you're a movie star – he's in his home office reading scripts or taking calls.

Mav told me he wants to begin producing movies. From what I've seen, producing means spending a whole lot of time phoning actors and cajoling them to star in the movie you're producing. I'd rather spend the day wrestling with the mini pigs in the mud bath than talking on the phone with spoiled actors, but Mav seems to enjoy it.

I find him exactly where I thought I would – in his home office. His back is to me as he stares out the window while he talks on the phone.

"I admit the role sounds interesting."

Role? Has Mav found the next movie he wants to star in? This I gotta hear. I don't make a sound as I sneak into the room and sit on his leather sofa.

"What's holding me back? One word. Quinn Wilder."

I slam my hand over my mouth before I can gasp out loud. Quinn Wilder? The woman he kissed for publicity? What does she have to do with the role? Oh no. Is he going to star in a movie with her?

Acid burns in my stomach. Quinn Wilder is everything I'm not. She's a glamourous movie star who probably wakes up gorgeous. I'm a hick from a small town who often forgets to brush her hair and comes home covered in animal dung more often than I prefer to admit.

"I'm not complaining about Quinn's acting capabilities." He huffs out a breath of air. "I realize this is a roll of a lifetime." A grunt. "There'll be other rolls." A sigh. "Let me think it over."

He hangs up and his chin falls to his chest as he rubs his neck.

Shit. Is his career in jeopardy because he doesn't want to work with Quinn Wilder? Is he doing this for me? Because I'm a jealous cow? Damn it. Do I have to swallow my jealousy to save his career?

He turns around to throw his phone on the desk and startles when he notices me.

"Hey, June Bug. I didn't realize you were home."

There's that word again. *Home.*

"I'm not."

His brow wrinkles. "You're not what?"

"I'm not home."

"What?"

"Do you need me to spell it for you? I am not home. My home is on the other side of town."

I don't know why I'm being obstinate. I blame hearing the name Quinn Walker come out of his mouth. Jealousy reared its ugly head and now nasty is exploding from my mouth. I know I need to chop the jealousy head off, but I don't exactly have a sword laying around for decapitating people or jealous rages.

"This is why I can't accept the part," he mumbles.

Wait. He's not accepting the part because we don't live together. Color me confused.

"This? What are you talking about? You may need to draw me a map."

He sits on the sofa next to me and grasps my hands. "You're not secure in our relationship."

I rear back. "I am. I love you. I know you love me."

"Then, why haven't you moved in?"

"Maybe because you never asked me."

He huffs. "How much more obvious do I need to make it? I gave you an entire chest of drawers, a closet, and a key. What else do you need? A personal invitation?"

"A girl likes to be asked."

He slides off the sofa and kneels before me. "Juniper Berry West, love of my life, most stubborn woman in the world, will you move in with me?"

"One, I'm not the most stubborn woman in the world. Have you met my sister, Ellery?"

He squeezes my hands. "I'm being serious."

I raise a brow. "Which is why you knelt on the floor to ask me to move in?"

He nods. "Yes."

I chew on my bottom lip as I contemplate him. "Are you asking me now because you're afraid I'm going to go apeshit when you accept a part in a movie with Quinn Wilder?"

"You heard me, did you?"

"Yep. And I'm not apologizing for eavesdropping. Your door was open." I glare down at him daring him to try.

"I'm not asking you to apologize. You live here. You can walk into my office whenever you want. I have nothing to hide from you."

"Except I do not, in fact, live here."

"Why not?"

"I told you why not. You never asked me to."

He sighs before standing and sitting in the chair across from me. "I just asked you. Did you forget already? Are you going senile in your old age?"

I stick my tongue out at him. "Did you forget you're four years older than me?"

He puffs out his chest. "Men get better with age."

"And women don't?"

"We're getting off track here."

"Said by every single man in the world when he realizes he's losing an argument to a woman."

"June Bug, I love you and I want you to move in. What do you say?"

"I say you only asked me because I overhead you discussing a role in a movie with Quinn Wilder." I can't help it. I spit her name out.

"I already refused the role."

"What?" I shriek. "It's the role of a lifetime."

He shrugs. "There will be other roles. Hopefully, without Quinn Wilder in them."

I jump to my feet and begin pacing the room. What a complete shit show. I'm damned if I do and damned if I don't. If I tell Mav to accept the roll, jealousy is going to eat at me. If I let him refuse the roll, I'll be *that* woman. The one who doesn't trust her man around other women. Dang it. I don't want to be her.

I whirl around and face him. "Accept the part."

He grasps my hands. "If you're uncomfortable with me working with Quinn Wilder, I don't want the part."

"I'm trying to be a better person here. Let me!"

He chuckles. "And I'm not spending three to four months shooting a movie with a woman you're not comfortable with me being around."

"Do you have feelings for Quinn Wilder?"

"She's a nice person, but I have no desire to be with her in a romantic way."

I believe him, damnit. Time to be a better woman. "Will you promise me one thing?"

He doesn't hesitate to respond, "I'll promise you the world."

My eyes itch. Stupid hay fever. Never mind I've never had hay fever or allergies of any kind before in my life.

"Stop being sweet."

"Sorry, June Bug. If there's one thing I can't promise you, it's to stop being sweet to you."

I narrow my eyes on him. "You're not helping matters."

He widens his eyes and feigns innocence. Whatever.

"Will you promise me if things change?" I have to pause to swallow the huge potato that suddenly lodged itself in my throat. "If you develop romantic feelings for Quinn, you'll tell me before you act on them?"

He growls. "Never gonna happen."

"This is not you promising me."

His hold on my hands tightens. "I, Maverick Langston, promise you, Juniper Berry West, aka June Bug, if I lose my ever-loving mind and develop romantic feelings for Quinn, I will not act on those feelings and I will let you know."

I allow his words to fill my heart before I inhale a deep breath and blow it out. "Okay, Maverick Langston. I want you to accept the part."

He holds my gaze for several seconds before nodding. "You realize this means I need to fly out to LA this week to meet with my agent and sign the contract?"

"I understand."

His eyes light up. "I have an idea. Why don't you come with me?"

"I can't. I don't have anyone to mind the animals."

"What about Harmony?"

I shake my head. "I don't want her handling the refuge for more than two days at a time, and I assume you need more than two days."

He frowns. "I do. I'll be gone for at least a week. As long as I'm flying out, I might as well get a few things handled with the sale of my house."

I cringe when he mentions selling his house. "You don't have to sell your house in Hollywood for me." I don't want to be the bitch who forces him to sell his house.

"There's no sense keeping it when my home base is now Winter Falls."

"You're sure?"

"I am. As long as you're sure you can handle me acting in a film with Quinn."

"I'm sure."

I hope I sound more confident than I feel because my confidence is wavering. I do believe Mav loves me and doesn't intend to hurt me. I also believe things happen when you're away from home for an extended period of time. Being in love with a movie star is not all it's cracked up to be.

Chapter 32

The more people I get to know, the more I love my dogs.

"Oh, Juniper. Wherefore art thou, Juniper?"

I lift my head from where I'm measuring the feed for the fennec foxes and glance over to find Ashlyn strolling toward me. "I'm standing in front of you. What are you doing here?"

Ashlyn avoids the Wildlife Refuge like the plague. Despite living with me and my animals for the year after she came home upon graduating college, my baby sister is not what I'd refer to as an animal lover. At most, she tolerates animals.

"I'm here to take your mind off of your troubles."

I narrow my eyes on her. "What troubles?"

"Please, don't try and deny it. I know you're bummed Rickie went to LA without you. You must be missing him."

I wish missing him was my sole problem. I'm trying hard to have faith in him and our relationship, but it's difficult when I'm confronted with pictures of him all over the entertainment news. He looks like the glamorous movie star he is.

I frown down at the threadbare and filthy coveralls I'm wearing. What the hell is he doing with me? And why is it so fricking hard to switch off the entertainment news?

"Is everyone calling him Rickie now?" I ask because I don't want to talk about my insecurities.

Ashlyn wouldn't understand. Her and insecure are not friends. They're not even acquaintances. The woman never wavered in her belief she could make Rowan love her. Judging by the ring on her finger and the baby in her belly, she was right.

"It's easier to keep fans off his trail if we call him Rickie."

My hands fist. "Fans. Are they in Winter Falls again? Do I need to grab my pitchfork?" I mentally add 'buy pitchfork' to my to-do list.

She waves away my concerns. "No need for your pitchfork yet."

"Your idea of getting my 'mind off my troubles' is reminding me of Mav's fans?"

My baby sister's mind works in mysterious ways. I've given up trying to understand her.

"No. Duh." She rolls her eyes. "I'm here to escort you to a cake tasting."

My ears perk up at the word 'cake'. Nevertheless, I have to ask, "Cake tasting? Why are we tasting cake?"

"Ellery wants to try out some flavors for her wedding."

I raise my eyebrows. "We're tasting cake for Ellery's wedding? Aspen is going to lose her mind."

She smirks. "I know."

"You didn't tell Aspen why we're meeting, did you?"

"Do I look like an amateur to you?"

"Do I have time to shower and change?"

Her nose wrinkles. "Not only do you have time. I'm going to have to insist you change before you step inside of *Bake Me Happy*."

"Rowan's making the cake?" *Bake Me Happy* is his bakery.

"Of course, my husband is making the cake. Is there another fabulous baker in Winter Falls I don't know about?"

I don't bother responding to her question. "Let me get changed."

My office at the Wildlife Refuge has a bathroom complete with a shower and bathtub. I quickly shower before dressing in the clothes I wore to work.

"I'm ready!" I holler as I exit my office.

I find Ashlyn leaning over the fence by the llamas.

"You know llamas spit," I say as I come up behind her.

She startles and nearly topples over the fence. "I swear your goal in life is to scare the crap out of me."

"It's good to have goals," I say as I follow her to her golf cart.

When we pull up to the bakery five minutes later, Aspen, Lilac, and Ellery are already waiting for us.

"I want to be supportive when one of my sisters is heartbroken, but I don't think eating your misery is a good idea," Lilac says as soon as we stop.

Ashlyn pats me on the back. "She's not heartbroken."

"Then, why are we at a bakery?" Lilac asks as she motions to the storefront.

Ashlyn bounces on her toes. "To taste test wedding cakes, of course!"

Lilac's brow wrinkles in confusion. "But you're already married."

"It's not for me. It's for Ellery."

"You have got to be kidding me!" Aspen explodes. "No way! I will not allow another sister to get married before me."

"What are you? The wedding police?" Ellery asks.

Aspen growls and gets in her face. "In this family, I am."

Ellery shrugs. "All you have to do is set a date and get married."

"Yeah, big sis. You've been engaged since the fall. What's the holdup?" I ask. Ashlyn was right. This is a great way to get my mind off 'things'.

"I want everything to be perfect."

Lilac reaches forward and grasps Aspen's hand. My mouth drops open. Lilac doesn't touch people unless she has to.

"Life is not perfect. It's full of ups and downs, surprises, and twists you never saw coming. If you love Lyric and want to be his wife, make it happen. Don't wait for perfect because it will never happen."

Now, my mouth is hanging open. When did Lilac become smart about people stuff?"

Ellery finds her voice first. "Hell, Aspen. If Lilac's saying you should get married, you better do it."

"Since we've got Aspen sorted, it's time to go taste some cake," Ashlyn says and skips to the entrance.

We follow her inside. *Bake Me Happy* is usually closed this late in the afternoon, but there's a table set for five in the middle of the room.

"Where is my baking god?" Ashlyn hollers before dashing around the counter and into the kitchen area.

"We might as well get comfortable. She may be a while," Ellery says before sitting down. "Is it rude to put my feet up on an empty chair? I promise to clean it before I leave."

Lilac frowns at her. "Why are your feet swollen? You're no longer pregnant."

"Who said anything about my feet being swollen? My feet are killing me from being on them all day."

"What kind of cakes did Rowan bake?" I ask Ellery who shrugs in reply.

"I gave him free rein."

"Can we forget about the cake for a minute and discuss Juniper's problem first?" Aspen's words may form a question, but she's not asking.

Lilac's nose wrinkles. "I thought you said she wasn't heart-broken."

"Ashlyn said she wasn't heartbroken. I want to hear it from the horse's mouth." When I don't speak, Aspen pokes me, "Well?"

"I'm not a horse."

She shoots lasers out of her eyes at me. "You know what I mean."

"I'm not heartbroken."

She purses her lips in disbelief. "Say it like you mean it."

"I'm serious. I'm not heartbroken."

"If not, why are you wearing your *I hate the world* t-shirt?"

I glance down at my t-shirt. "It doesn't say *I hate the world.*"

"You only wear your UC t-shirt when you're mad at the world."

Crap. How does she know? "You pay way too much attention to what I wear."

"And you're avoiding the question."

Yes. Yes, I am. "Fine," I huff. "I'm not heartbroken."

"I get it," Ellery pipes up. "I worried about Cole and what he was doing in Chicago when I wasn't there with him."

We all know how much of a problem she had with Cole being out of town. She nearly ditched the father of her child, the man she loves, because she couldn't deal with him being an out-of-towner. Life would be much easier if my issue with Mav was he wasn't born in Winter Falls.

"At least, you didn't have to see Cole on the cover of every glossy magazine ever printed and all over social media," I grumble.

"I would hate that," Ellery admits.

"Do you not trust him?" Lilac asks. "I can hack into the security system of the restaurants he frequents and check he isn't cheating on you."

"Can you really?"

"It's not difficult."

Wait. What am I thinking? I'm not going to allow my sister to cyberstalk my boyfriend. I might be a jealous cow, but I'm not a crazy stalker.

"Thank you for the offer, Lilac, but I'm going to decline at this moment."

"Good." Aspen nods in approval. "You should trust the man you love."

"I'm trying," I whisper. "I'm trying."

It helps Mav phones me every night and tells me all about his day. He also sends messages throughout the day. They aren't long – the guy is busy after all – but it's enough for me to know he's thinking about me.

Ashlyn skips out of the kitchen, followed by Rowan who's carrying a cake. "Did you get her sorted?"

Get me sorted. What is this? A therapy cake tasting? "Can all of you stop butting into my life now? I want to eat cake."

Rowan holds one up. "This is red velvet. I thought we'd start with something traditional and move on from there."

I mouth *thank you* to him and he winks.

Phew. I've successfully maneuvered my way out of this uncomfortable conversation with my sisters. This is what I get for being close with them. There are no boundaries when it comes to the West sisters. Frankly, I wouldn't have it any other way. No matter how much I want to throw them all in the capybara's pool at the moment.

Chapter 33

My dogs weren't chasing people on bikes. They don't even own bikes.

"What's going on?" I ask Lilac when I enter the town hall where I've been summoned. "The monthly business meeting isn't until next week."

"This is an extraordinary meeting." Lilac the literal strikes again.

"Yes, I understand it's an extraordinary meeting. The question is why we're having one." There's only one reason I can think of for there to be an extraordinary meeting. "Is it because of the money we found?"

"You mean the loot," Ashlyn corrects.

I roll my eyes. Someone has a flare for the dramatic. Obviously. There's a reason she studied drama at college after all.

"Excuse me. Because of the loot we found?"

"Among other things," Lilac says, and Ashlyn elbows her.

"What?" Lilac asks.

"I thought you understood human emotions after your little speech to Aspen the other day."

My gaze ping pongs between them. They're up to something. I cross my arms over my chest. "What's going on?"

Ashlyn bats her eyelashes at me. "Whatever do you mean?"

Rowan arrives and throws an arm around her shoulders. "You oversold it, Dream girl."

She pushes him away. "It's Mayor Dream girl to you."

An alarm goes off and she fishes her phone out of her pocket before switching it off. "Time for the Queen to perform her duties."

She glides to the front of the room as if she's royalty, but as soon as she's standing in front of everyone, she fists a gavel before slamming it down on the table with an amount of force, which is anything but regal.

"Is she trying to pound a hole into the table or what?" Ellery asks as she sits down next to me. Aspen sits on the other side of me while Lilac joins Ashlyn at the front of the room.

"Where's Willow?"

Ellery points behind her to where Mom is cuddling her granddaughter. "I swear Mom spends more time with her than I do."

"Don't worry. Once Ashlyn pops her baby out and Juniper gets pregnant, Mom will have to split her time."

I smack Aspen on the arm. "I told you Mav and I want to wait to have children."

She shrugs. "This one," she indicates Ellery, "wasn't planning on having a baby either."

"True story," Ellery agrees.

My mouth opens, and I blurt out things I should keep to myself. "I'm not sold on the idea of having a child with a movie star. He'll be gone all the time doing who knows what. I'm barely used to the idea of being attached to someone famous myself." And trying to convince myself I can handle it.

"I have a feeling you're going to change your mind soon," Aspen says.

"I agree."

I narrow my eyes as I look back and forth between the two of them. What's up with my sisters today? "What are you talking about?"

Aspen widens her eyes in a display of innocence. I'm not buying it.

The lights dim. "What's going on now?"

"Just watch and all will be revealed," she sings.

Winter Falls is known for pulling hijinks, but usually I'm in on it. I don't enjoy being left out. Plus, it's never a good sign when you're the one left out. I eye the emergency exit. Can I make it there before I'm tackled by my sisters if I need to escape?

"The only thing revealed thus far is I don't like you very much right now," I grumble.

A screen rolls down from the ceiling. "When did we get a screen in the town hall?"

"When we struck it rich after we found the bandit's loot," Ashlyn answers from the front of the room.

We haven't maneuvered all the legalities of the found money yet and she's already spending it. I pity whoever takes the mayor position over from her next year.

"Roll the film!"

Wait. Roll the film? It's not movie night. And movie night is at the library where the seats are more comfortable. And I'm in charge of movie night. I try to stand but Aspen and Ellery grab my arms to hold me down. So much for making it to the emergency exit.

"You need to watch this," Aspen says.

"You really need to watch this," Ellery agrees.

I slump in my chair. "Whatever."

The screen lights up and the opening credits for *The Breakfast Show* begin. "Are we watching the morning news?"

This is getting weirder and weirder.

"Just wait," Ashlyn says as she sits in our row and passes out beers.

"What are you doing? You're pregnant and Ellery's breastfeeding. I think we can do without the beer."

"I could use a beer," Lilac mutters as she places the bottle to her lips and drinks.

"What's going on with her?" I whisper my question to Aspen.

"Nope. You first. We'll deal with Lilac later."

"Me? I don't have any issues." Damn. I should have tried harder to escape.

Ellery snorts. "Uh-huh. Wasn't it you who admitted not more than five minutes ago you're worried about having children with a movie star?"

This is why I prefer animals to humans. Animals don't talk back. They shed a shit ton and need to be let out at all times of the day and night, but they don't talk back.

"Fast forward to the good part," Sage orders from the back of the room.

Oh boy. If Sage knows what the good part is, I'm pretty certain I won't enjoy whatever I'm about to watch.

"You're going to love this," Aspen says as if she can read my mind.

Maybe I could use a beer, too. I take a fortifying drink.

"Stop! This is it!" Ashlyn shouts, and the show begins again.

A male and female host – I have no idea what their names are since I don't usually watch this show unless Mav is on it – are smiling at the camera before the woman announces, "Joining us today is our favorite romantic comedy star. None other than Maverick Langston."

I frown. Mav didn't tell me he was in New York today. But yet there he is, strutting onto the set with his Hollywood smile secure on his face.

"He's here to talk about his upcoming movie with Quinn Wilder."

His smile drops as he sits down across from the hosts of the show.

The male host lowers his voice, "Rumor has it love is in the air between Mav and his co-star."

I hear someone growl before I realize it's me. I'm the one growling. I sip on my beer and hope no one noticed my behavior.

Mav clears his throat. "Actually."

The other host nods and charges on as if Mav hadn't spoken. "I heard they were seen being all cozy at a restaurant in LA."

I grunt, and Ellery pats my arm. "It gets better."

How does she know? Wait a minute. I know what's going on. I stand and shout my question to the room, "Has everyone in town seen this?"

"Yes!" The crowd replies as hands fly into the air.

"How did I miss it?"

The footage pauses while I wait for an answer.

"Maybe because you had to rush out to the refuge to deal with a sick llama this morning?" Ashlyn's statement sounds more like a question.

"Please tell me you didn't poison my llama so I missed this interview. Do you know how much time I spent collecting stool samples for the vet today?"

She shivers. "No. And I don't want to." Yep. Ashlyn definitely poisoned my llama.

"You're lucky llama poop has no odor, or your pregnancy wouldn't hold me back," I grumble at her as I plop down in my seat again.

She beams a smile at me. "Hurrah for no odor llama poop. Roll the film!"

The recording begins again, and I can't help myself. I lean forward in my chair to watch closer. I'm riveted to the sight of Mav on the screen.

"It's true." Mav nods. "Quinn and I did have dinner together, but we're anything but cozy. We're not romantically involved." He stares into the camera. "Our relationship is purely platonic."

Cheers erupt around me. Why are they cheering? Everyone in town knows the 'kiss' was a publicity stunt.

The female host waggles her eyebrows. "Are you positive? The Hollywood rumor mill is alight with speculation about Maverick Langston being in love."

He grins. "I am in love." He appears happy and my pulse speeds up. What is he doing?

The male host addresses the camera. "You heard it here first, folks. Maverick Langston is officially off the market."

The female host leans closer. Geez. If she leans any further, she'll be sitting in Mav's lap. "And who is the lucky lady? Anyone we know?"

"Actually, it's not. Juniper isn't interested in Hollywood and all its trappings."

I gasp and forget how to breathe. He said my name. My name! On national television! Holy cows have come home! He outed our relationship.

"She sounds intriguing. When do we get to meet her?"

Mav shrugs off the question. "I have a different surprise for you today."

She leans back against the sofa. "I don't know if we can handle another surprise today." She's not the only one I think as I clutch my neck and gasp for breath.

"You're not going to want to miss this surprise. It's a good one." He winks.

"Well, I'm interested if she's not." The male host elbows his co-host.

"I was hoping you'd let me sing a song I wrote for Juniper."

"When did he record a song?" I ask the room.

Ashlyn whistles and studies her feet.

"Ashlyn," I growl.

"He swore me to secrecy."

"I think it's safe to say the secret is out."

"The secret about you and Rickie being in love is definitely out. Juniper and Rickie sitting in a tree."

I smack a hand over her mouth before she can continue with the stupid childish song. Besides, I want to hear Mav sing. I've heard him sing in the shower, but I had no idea he was interested in music. I've seen the guitars at his house, too, but I assumed they were collector items.

Someone dashes onto the screen and hands Mav a guitar. "This is for my June Bug," he says as he strums the strings. "It's called Stay For Forever."

I'm fixated on the screen as Mav sings along with his acoustic guitar. He sings about falling in love with a stubborn woman, about making mistakes and almost losing her, about never wanting to let her go, and about wanting to build a family with her.

By the time the song finishes, I'm a puddle of melted goo on the floor. Here I was worried about Mav being away. I'm an idiot. It's time to stop worrying and start living. And all my living will be done with Maverick in his house from here on out.

Chapter 34

I don't need an animal to awaken my soul, I have my June Bug and all her animals.

MAVERICK

I frown when I switch on my phone and notice I don't have any missed calls from Juniper. I messaged her before I got on the plane to let her know I'd be home tonight. I thought she'd be excited as I'm coming home a few days earlier than planned. Maybe she missed my message?

I dial her number as I walk to my car. I listen to the phone ring and ring. I don't think she's going to pick up, but she finally does on the sixth ring.

"Mav." She's breathing heavy.

"Are you running?"

"Ha! No. Me, run?" Except she can't catch her breath.

"What are you doing then?"

"Me? I'm … uh… working?"

"Why do you sound uncertain about what you're doing?"

A crash sounds and Juniper swears. "Shit. I gotta go. Love you."

"Love you," I repeat but she already hung up.

This is not the welcome home I expected after my big reveal on *The Breakfast Show*. Maybe I overdid it? Maybe Juniper's mad I told the world I'm in love with her? But she was mad before when I didn't tell my fans about her.

I shake my head. Women. I'll never understand them.

I spend the two-hour drive from the airport developing and discarding plans on how to win Juniper back if she's upset about what I did. When I arrive in Winter Falls, I still have no idea what to say. I thought she'd be happy I told the world I'm no longer single.

I contemplate driving straight to Juniper's house, but I've been traveling for eight hours. I need a shower and some clean clothes before I confront her.

I frown when I pull up to my house and note the golf carts and bikes parked everywhere. I rub a hand down my face as I consider switching the engine back on and making my way to Juniper's house after all. I'm not in the mood for a Winter Falls invasion when things with my woman are up in the air.

I expect to find the entire town crammed into my living room, but when I open the door Juniper is standing alone in the room. Her face is flushed and there's sweat on her brow. I rush to her.

"What's wrong? Are you sick? Come on. I'll drive you to the emergency room."

She bats away my hands. "Um. Hello to you, too. I'm not sick. I'm sweaty from working hard."

I haul her into my arms. She tries to pull away, but I don't let her.

"I don't care if you're sweaty. I haven't seen you in ten days. I need you in my arms to remind me you're real."

"Of course, I'm real. This is not a dreamscape from *Inception*."

"Smart ass," I mutter before my lips crash on hers. She sighs and I use the opportunity to thrust my tongue into her mouth. It's been too long since I tasted her flavor of strawberries and wilderness. Strawberries have always been my favorite fruit, but they've never tasted as good as her mouth does.

She throws her arms around me and draws me near until there's no space left between our bodies. I press my hardness against her stomach, and she moans into my mouth. *Yes.* I hook her leg under my arm to open her to me.

Bang! Bang! Bang!

I wrench my lips from Juniper's and glance across the room to the patio doors where Feather is waving at me.

"Can I use the restroom before your clothes come off?"

"Their clothes are coming off?" Sage shoves Feather out of the way. "I want to see."

"Me too!" Petal shouts.

Soon enough all of the Gossip gals are peering into the house through my patio doors.

I drop Juniper's leg and place my forehead against hers as I catch my breath. Once I've got my body under control, I glance toward the doors and open my mouth to tell Feather she can use the downstairs half-bath, but the words die in my throat when I notice the doggy bowls on the floor in the kitchen.

I release Juniper and stalk to the kitchen. The changes aren't limited to the addition of doggy bowls on the floor, there's also a red mixer and matching toaster on the counter.

The gossip gals and their restroom needs are forgotten as I prowl through the downstairs of my house. The couch in the living room is now adorned with throw blankets and pillows. There are books and knick-knacks on the previously empty bookshelves. Finally, there are placements and a centerpiece on the dining room table.

"What's going on?"

Juniper bites her lip. "I moved in?"

I stalk to her and grasp her hands. "You moved in?"

She shrugs. "You said you wanted me to."

I hate how uncertain she sounds. I squeeze her hands. "I do want you to live with me. I'd get down on my knee and ask you to marry me right here, right now, but I know I need to prove to you I'm here to stay before I propose."

"I think I figured out you're here to stay when you announced you're in love with Juniper on the most watched morning television program in America."

"You're not mad I kept your full name and the town secret?" This is the only theory I could come up with to explain why she would be angry with me.

She snorts. "Um, no. One run-in with your rabid fans was enough for me."

"They weren't rabid."

She lifts an eyebrow. "Right. They were completely normal."

"I can't keep your name and this town secret forever. Eventually, people will find out."

"I know. I'm not saying I'm not going to freak out the first time one of those paparazzi print a picture of me covered in llama dung, but I'll deal."

I growl. "No, you won't. I'll deal with the press."

"Hey!" She pokes me in the chest. "We're supposed to be partners. We'll deal with any press challenges together."

I capture her hand before she can poke me again. "I know we're partners, but partners can split tasks. I'll leave you to handle the animals. I assume you've brought all your creatures here to live with us as well?"

"Except Dale. I know he freaks you out."

I will never admit it, but the little chipmunk definitely freaks me out.

Juniper giggles at my silent admission. "Forest took him. He was missing his brother Chip anyway."

"And Meowise is here somewhere?"

She cringes. "Fingers crossed she's not leaving presents for you in your shoes."

I sigh. "I'll buy new ones." For my June Bug, I'll do anything. Including tell the press where to shove it when they invade her privacy. "We have a deal then? You'll handle the animals, and I'll handle the press."

"Fine." She gives in. "But if anyone approaches me in person, I'm handling it my way."

"I'll warn the press about your penchant for flinging animal poop," I tease.

"You throw poop at a person one time," she mutters as she grins up at me and my heart warms. Home. I'm home. I don't mean the house we're standing in, I mean Juniper – she's my home.

I grin. "Does this mean you're ready for me to propose?" I start to kneel, and she squeals as she stops me.

"Hold on, big guy. I moved in with you five minutes ago. Literally, we finished moving my stuff in seconds before you arrived. You could have warned me you were coming home early."

Now I understand why she was out of breath when I phoned.

"It wouldn't have been a surprise if I warned you, now, would it?"

She smirks. "Instead, I surprised you." She lifts her arms in the air. "Surprise! I moved in!"

I pick her up and twirl her around. "Welcome home, June Bug."

My gaze lands on her mouth but before my lips can meet hers someone bangs on the patio doors again.

"I wasn't kidding about needing the restroom," Feather says.

"What's wrong with you?" Sage huffs. "They were about to give us a show and you interrupted them. For the second time, I might add."

"Why don't you go pee in the forest like a normal person?" Cayenne asks.

"Because we're not all yoga instructors. I don't fancy my knees giving out while I'm squatting and having the fire department come save me while my pants are down."

"I don't know why not. River is dreamy." Petal sighs.

"You would know. He's come to your house often enough after you 'accidentally' started a fire with all of your candles."

Petal frowns at Sage. "You're supposed to keep the calls you receive as police dispatcher confidential."

Clove bursts out laughing. "When has Sage ever kept anything confidential?"

"Who cares about confidential?" Everyone except Sage apparently. "Project MavBerry is a success. We did it again!"

The Gossip gals high-five each other. I chuckle at their antics as I motion for Feather to come inside. She opens the door, and I hear a crowd outside. I cock an eyebrow at Juniper in question.

"This is also your welcome to Winter Falls party."

Ah, yes. I nearly forgot about the golf carts in my driveaway and the bikes in my front yard. "I've lived in Winter Falls for years."

"But now you're not here to stay for a while. You're here to stay for forever."

"I most certainly am, June Bug. I most certainly am." I lean my forehead against hers. "I love you."

"And I love you, even if you are a big Hollywood star."

I chuckle. Only my June Bug would hold it against me for being a star.

She glances outside where I can hear people laughing and music playing. "We should probably join the party. It is on your behalf after all."

I waggle my eyebrows. "Do we have to?"

She grasps my hand. "Yeah, we do. Because I'm not having sex with you in the house while everyone parties outside."

"No one has to know what we're doing."

"I'll know," Feather says as she shuffles out of the bathroom toward the backdoor.

Juniper shrugs. "Welcome to Winter Falls."

I squeeze her hand. "It's good to be home."

Winter Falls with all its quirks and characters and crazy environmental rules is the first place I ever felt at home. I don't plan to live anywhere else ever again. I do plan to convince Juniper to marry me and have my children as soon as possible, though.

Chapter 35

Grumpy – a term often used interchangeably with asshole

LILAC

"Another one bites the dust. Good job." Aspen pats her own back.

I frown at her. "What do you mean? Good job? You did not bring Juniper and Maverick together."

She snorts. "Of course, I did."

Ashlyn skips over to us. "What are we gossiping about?"

"About how pregnant women shouldn't skip."

I frown at Aspen. "I don't know where you heard this information. Pregnant women can skip."

Ashlyn throws her arms around me, and I pat her back awkwardly. It's not that I don't like to touch people. I don't have haphephobia aka an intense fear of being touched. I just never got the gist of how to properly engage in affection.

As soon as my family noticed how uncomfortable I was with affection, they backed off. I love them for trying to make me feel more comfortable, but their backing off had the opposite effect. Now, I'm unsure how to provide or accept affection.

"Are we discussing how to matchmake Lilac yet?" Ellery asks as she joins us.

I retreat a few steps, but before I can escape, Ashlyn shackles my wrist. "Nuh-uh. No running away."

I purse my lips. "I wasn't running away."

She rolls her eyes. "It's like you don't realize we've lived with you all of your life and know you through and through."

"You haven't lived with me all of my life, since I'm older than you," I correct her.

I know. I know. I should stop being literal, but I can't help it. When someone makes a statement, which is incorrect, my mouth opens and I correct them before I can stop myself. Frankly, I don't know if I want to stop myself. False information is bad. And I do mean bad in the worst way imaginable. Spreading false information can literally start wars.

"I don't think we need to worry about matchmaking Lilac," Aspen says in a singsong voice.

I blow out a breath of relief. "Good. Can we switch to a topic worthy of discussing now?"

Ellery taps her chin. "I agree. I believe she already has her eye on someone."

I rear back. "What are you talking about? I'm not dating anyone."

"But you're not having your sexual liaisons anymore either, are you?" Ashlyn asks.

I should have never confessed my custom of having a sexual partner with whom I have relations at lunchtime on occasion to them. My sisters have decided my idea of non-committal sex is seedy.

There's nothing seedy about it. I make the acquaintance of a man I find attractive. We discuss having a sexual rendezvous without any commitment and then we carry forward. We even meet in a nice hotel, not a motel.

But Ashlyn's right. I haven't had a sexual partner for a while now. When my new boss joined the environmental engineering firm I work at, my workload doubled to the point I don't remember the last time I took a lunch break.

I'm exaggerating. I have the information about my last lunch break stored in my agenda. I store all dates and events in my agenda. Everyone should. It's quite handy for future reference.

"My having or not having sexual liaisons has nothing to do with you."

Ashlyn tilts her head back and barks out a laugh. She laughs and laughs until she has to wrap an arm around her belly. "Priceless!"

"What's priceless? And why are you laughing?"

"Duh." She snorts. "Because everything you do has to do with me. With us."

Aspen threads her arm through mine. "I don't know why you're confused. This is the way it's always been with the West sisters."

Yes, well, until Aspen came home I could escape into my work. Since she came home last summer, however, I've somehow lost the ability to escape.

The crowd quiets down. "Are Juniper and Maverick finally coming outside?" I ask as I peer toward the back of their house.

"Nope." Ashlyn pops the p in the word, which is usually a sign she's up to no good.

"Why is everyone quieting down? Is someone going to make an announcement?"

I study Aspen. Could she be pregnant? I noticed Ellery and Ashlyn were pregnant long before anyone else. Could I have missed the signs with Aspen? Of course, I haven't. She's holding a beer.

Ellery points across the yard. "I think everyone's waiting to hear what he has to say."

I look to where she's pointing and scowl. What is he doing here? It's bad enough I can barely get away from him during the workday. I should be able to have some privacy during my free time.

I don't wait for him to find me. I march across the yard. "What are you doing here?" I demand of Beckett Dempsey, my boss.

"I was about to ask you the same thing."

"You have no right to ask about my whereabouts when it's not related to work," I remind him of a fact I've reminded him of several times before.

He rubs a hand down his face. "When you refused to answer my calls, I thought you were on a date."

"I refused to answer your calls because I am not at your beck and call despite what you may believe."

"You rushed out of the office in a hurry. I thought there was a problem."

I cross my arms. "I did not rush out of the office. I completed my tasks for the day and left."

"You didn't check with me before leaving."

I count to ten before I lash out at him. He may be annoying and out of line, but he's still my boss. *Clean Mountain Environment*, the firm I work at, is the only environmental engineering firm within driving distance of Winter Falls. If I want to stay living in this town – and I do – I can't get fired from my position no matter how annoying my boss is.

"I didn't realize checking with you was a requirement before leaving for the day."

"Go get him, Lilac!" Ashlyn shouts from behind me.

Beckett glances past me to nod to my sister. "Who is she?"

"She is none of your business. My private life is none of your business. I concede you are my boss."

He snorts. "How gracious of you."

"But being my boss does not entitle you to information about my private life. I'd prefer it if you left now."

Ashlyn skips over to us. "Hi." She holds out her hand. "I'm Ashlyn."

When he reaches forward to shake her hand, she uses the hold to drag him further into the yard. "We're having a party. Come join us. I'll introduce you to everyone."

I glare at my baby sister carting my boss off. I don't want him anywhere near my family. I don't care how gorgeous he is or how smart he is. He has complicated written all over him and I don't do complicated.

About the Author

D.E. Haggerty is an American who has spent the majority of her adult life abroad. She has lived in Istanbul, various places throughout Germany, and currently finds herself in The Hague. She has been a military policewoman, a lawyer, a B&B owner/operator and now a writer.